Jessie Becker ground her teeth in frustration at the tall, dark-skinned Ranger's threat.

She knew exactly why he was here, and she had about as much use for him as she had for the other Rangers and the sheriff who'd been traipsing all over her property the past few days.

No, she had no use for him. They'd brought out the big guns now. This one was Native American, a sexy, broad-shouldered, hunky one at that.

Her stomach fluttered with awareness, but she steeled herself against his accusations—and his sinful looks. The fringed rawhide jacket he wore gave him a rugged look that matched his brusque masculinity. Shoulder-length thick black hair brushed his neck and his eyes were the darkest color of brown she'd ever seen. Brown and sultry and mysterious.

They were also as cold and intimidating as his thick, husky voice.

He inched closer, so close his breath brushed her cheek. A breath that hinted at coffee and intimacy and…sex

RITA HERRON

RAWHIDE RANGER

HARLEQUIN®

TORONTO • NEW YORK • LONDON
AMSTERDAM • PARIS • SYDNEY • HAMBURG
STOCKHOLM • ATHENS • TOKYO • MILAN • MADRID
PRAGUE • WARSAW • BUDAPEST • AUCKLAND

To Sheila and Linda—friends, fans and cowboy lovers!

Recycling programs
for this product may
not exist in your area.

ISBN-13: 978-0-373-69459-4

RAWHIDE RANGER

Copyright © 2010 by Rita B. Herron

ABOUT THE AUTHOR

Award-winning author Rita Herron wrote her first book when she was twelve, but didn't think real people grew up to be writers. Now she writes so she doesn't have to get a *real* job. A former kindergarten teacher and workshop leader, she traded her storytelling to kids for romance, and now she writes romantic comedies and romantic suspense. She lives in Georgia with her own romance hero and three kids. She loves to hear from readers, so please write her at P.O. Box 921225, Norcross, GA 30092-1225, or visit her Web site at www.ritaherron.com.

Books by Rita Herron

CAST OF CHARACTERS

Sergeant Cabe Navarro—He's supposed to soothe ruffled feathers between the opposing factions in Comanche Creek and tie up the murder investigation…but Jessie Becker complicates everything.

Jessie Becker—Her father is a prime suspect in the murders, and she is determined to prove him innocent—but someone wants her dead.…

Jonah Becker—Is he a cold-blooded killer or just an unscrupulous businessman?

Trace Becker—Jonah's ruthless son and Jessie's brother. He put the original land deal together and would do anything to protect his daddy's money.

Woodrow "Woody" Sadler—The popular mayor who might have greased the way for Jonah to get the illegal land. Would he kill to protect his reputation?

Deputy Shane Tolbert—Did he kill his ex Marcie Turner, and the others, then try to frame someone else?

Charla Sadler—She sold the artifacts found on the sacred Native American burial grounds. How far would she go to cover her wrongdoing?

Jerry Collier—Head of the Comanche Creek land office. Is he killing to hide his illegal activity?

Ellie Penateka—A local Native American activist who had a one-night stand with Cabe. She will do anything for her cause.…

Prologue

"The case is not over," Ranger Lieutenant Wyatt Colter announced to the task force gathered in the courthouse in Comanche Creek. "We still have a murderer to catch."

Ranger Sergeant Cabe Navarro frowned. The last place in the world he wanted to be was back in his hometown. When he'd left it years ago, he'd sworn never to return.

But he couldn't disobey an order. And so far, the multiple murder case had been a mess. National media was starting to take interest, and if they didn't solve the case soon, the Rangers would be usurped by the FBI and look incompetent.

None of them wanted that.

Still, if they thought he could be a buffer between the Native Americans and Caucasians in town, they were sorely mistaken.

Cabe had never fit in either world.

Ranger Lieutenant Colter introduced the task force members. Forensic anthropologist Dr. Nina Jacobsen. Ranger Sergeant Livvy Hutton who absentmindedly rubbed her arm where she'd just recently been shot. And Reed Hardin, the sheriff of Comanche Creek.

Hardin cast a worried and protective look at Hutton, cementing the rumor that Cabe had heard that they had gotten involved on the case and now planned to marry.

"Okay," Wyatt said. "Let's recap the case so far. "First, two bodies were found on the Double B, Jonah Becker's ranch, property the Native Americans claim was stolen from them. The first body was Mason Lattimer, an antiquities dealer, the second, Ray Phillips, a Native American activist who claimed Becker stole the land from the Natives."

"They have proof?" Cabe asked.

"Supposedly there is evidence that suggests Billy Whitley forged paperwork to make it appear that the land originally belonged to Jonah Becker's great-great-grandfather. That paperwork overrode the Reston Act which had given the Natives ownership."

Cabe made a sound of disgust in his throat. "No wonder the Native Americans are up in arms."

Lieutenant Colter nodded, then continued, "Marcie James, who worked at the land office, had planned to testify against Jerry Collier, the lawyer who brokered the deal, but she went missing two years ago. Evidence indicated she was murdered and buried on the property and construction of the road going through was halted."

He paused. "But we now know Marcie faked her kidnapping and murder. She resurfaced though, but someone caught up with her, and killed her at a cabin on Becker's property."

Sheriff Hardin stood, a frown on his face. Cabe had

heard that Hardin was protective of his town and his job. "My deputy Shane Tolbert was found standing over Marcie's body holding a Ruger. He claimed he was knocked unconscious and someone put a gun in his hand. We arrested him, but forensics indicated that the blood spatter and fingerprints were consistent with his story, so he was released." Hardin rubbed a hand over the back of his neck. "But his father, Ben, was certain we were gunning to pin the crimes on his son, and tried to kill me and Sergeant Hutton."

"Ben Tolbert is in jail?" Cabe said.

"Yes. He copped to threatening us and destroying key evidence, as well as setting fire to the cabin where Marcie was murdered, but not to murder."

"Daniel Taabe, the leader of the Native American faction, was also murdered?" Cabe asked, knowing Taabe's death was the trigger for bringing him into the case. Everyone in town thought the Rangers were trying to cover up the crime.

"Right." Lieutenant Colter's eyes snapped with anger. "So far, our suspects include Jonah Becker, his son Trace, his lawyer Jerry Collier who brokered the land deal, the mayor Woody Sadler who could have been protecting Shane as Ben did, and possibly Charla Whitley, Billy Whitley's wife."

Holy hell. Half the town were suspects. Between that and the war raging between the Caucasian faction and Native American faction, he had his job cut out.

Especially since both sides detested him.

He'd get this case tied up as soon as possible, and leave town. And this time, nothing would bring him back.

Chapter One

Anxiety plucked at Cabe as he parked at the Double B where the murder victims' bodies had been found. He scanned the area, half expecting an ambush.

Someone had been sabotaging the investigation at every turn, and he had to be on guard every minute.

According to the lieutenant, Jonah Becker was furious at having the Rangers on his property. And he certainly wouldn't welcome Cabe in town or on his ranch.

Jonah had always made it clear that he thought the Comanches were beneath him.

Not that Cabe cared what the rich bastard thought. He'd dealt with prejudice all his life. Prejudice from both sides.

But his Native blood ran deep. So did his cop instincts.

And as he climbed from his SUV, the scent of death surrounded him.

According to Dr. Jacobsen, the forensic anthropologist brought in to study the bones of an unnamed cadaver that had also been found here, one grave held ancient bones belonging to a Native. That grave suggested that this land was a Native American sacred burial ground. Worse, the body had been *moved*.

Dr. Jacobsen was right.

The ancient war cries and whispers of the dead bombarded him as he walked across the dusty, rock-strewn rugged land. There were other graves here. Graves of Natives who'd been buried long ago. Spirits who were upset that their sacred grounds had been disturbed.

Noting the plywood platform the forensic anthropologist had built to excavate the first finds, he muttered a silent thanks that Dr. Jacobsen had respected the grounds.

The image of the most recent corpse in the morgue flashed back, jolting him to the past and the reason he'd left years ago. The way the legs had been bound with chord, the face painted red, the eyes glued shut with clay—all part of the Comanche burial ritual. Just the way Daniel Taabe's had been.

And exactly the way his little brother had been buried as well. Pain and grief suffused him. His little brother had died because his father had relied on the Big Medicine Ceremony to heal him instead of taking him to the hospital as Cabe had begged.

The moment they'd buried Simon, Cabe had left town, and he hadn't spoken to his father since.

Shaking off the bitter memories, he studied the area where the bodies of the antiquities dealer Mason Lattimer and Native American activist Ray Phillips had been discovered. Forensics had already combed the area and bagged everything they'd discovered. He didn't expect to find anything new, but took a few minutes to search himself. Yet as he touched his finger to the ground, a sense of violence and pain assaulted him full force.

He could always sense death. It was part of his Comanche heritage.

Now the stench, the anguish and suffering, the cries of the fallen Native Americans filled the air as if they still walked the land. He heard their footfalls, the stampeding horses, the screams of women and children and battle cries echoing from the ground. He saw their ghostly spirits gathering as one.

Their collective shouts that this land belonged to them.

With his gloved hand, he pushed aside a clump of thorny brush and pushed at the dirt below, then dug a sample of the clay from the ground. The lab could verify if it was the same clay used in the burial ritual.

"You're going to jail, Becker," he muttered. Tipping back his Stetson, he collected a sample and bagged it.

Horse hooves pounded against the ground, the sound coming closer. He glanced up, half expecting to see more spirits, but instead a woman wearing a black Stetson with silver trim approached, riding a palomino, her long curly red hair flowing in the wind.

Dammit. Jessie Becker, Jonah Becker's daughter. He'd heard about her, seen pictures of her. She was not only a knockout but supposedly the brains behind the ranch's recent rise in success.

And she hated the Rangers being on her land, had thwarted their attempts to interrogate her father, protecting him at every turn.

She galloped toward him, rage and anger spewing from her aura as she brought the horse to a halt barely inches from his side and glared down at him. The morning Texas sun was nearly blinding him, and he shifted his own Stetson to shade his eyes so he could see her more clearly.

God, she was a sight for sore eyes. Her nose was dainty, eyes a crystal shade of green like fresh spring grass, her body full of sexy curves. And those legs...

Her lean legs hugged the horse's flanks just the way they would a man.

His body tightened, his sex hardening against his fly.

Double damn. He didn't need or want to be attracted to the rancher, not when they were on opposite sides of the land issue—and perhaps the murders.

"What in the hell are you doing here?" she asked.

In spite of the anger in her voice, Cabe bit back a smile at her sassy tone. He hated pansy, whiny women and judging from her attitude—and the way she rode—she didn't fit that category.

But he had his priorities straight. His work as a Ranger. His people—the Comanches.

And women.

In that order.

The spitfire redhead giving him a go-to-hell look was a complication. But now the damn sex kitten—rather, tigress—was part of the job, part of the task force the Rangers had put together, and he had to deal with her.

He stood to his full six-four and pasted on his most intimidating stare. "Sergeant Cabe Navarro," he said. "I'm investigating the recent murders."

She slid one leg over the side of the palomino and dismounted as if she'd been born in the saddle, then planted her hands on her hips and squared her shoulders. Still, her head barely came to his chest, and he could pick her up with one hand tied behind his back.

"When are you Rangers going to stop harassing my family?" she barked.

His gaze settled over her, intense and suspicious. Since the Rangers had arrived, she'd been more or less the spokesperson for the Becker family. What was she hiding?

"When we find the evidence we need to put away your father for stealing Native American property." He paused for emphasis. "And for murder."

JESSIE BECKER GROUND HER teeth in frustration at the tall, dark-skinned Ranger's threat. She knew exactly why he was here, and she had about as much use for him as she had for the other Rangers and the sheriff who'd been traipsing all over her property the past few days.

No, she had *no* use for him. They'd brought out the big guns now. This one was Native American, a sexy broad-shouldered hunky one at that. But his heritage meant that he would definitely be out to slaughter her family.

And her as well.

She had to protect her family.

"My father didn't steal this land, and he certainly never killed anyone." Her tone matched his, and she dug the silver toe of her boot into the dirt.

"Are you sure about that, Miss Becker? Maybe you don't know your father as well as you think." He stepped closer, tilted his head sideways and pierced her with his laser eyes. "Or maybe you're covering for him."

Her stomach fluttered with awareness, but she steeled

herself against his accusations—and his sinful looks. The fringed rawhide jacket he wore gave him a rugged look that matched his brusque masculinity. Shoulder-length, thick black hair brushed his neck and his eyes were the darkest color of brown she'd ever seen. Brown and sultry and mysterious.

They were also as cold and intimidating as his thick, husky voice.

Both of which could melt the clothes right off a woman. Even *hers* and she was a hard sell when it came to men.

But she had to stay on her toes and couldn't let down her guard—or her bra straps—for a second.

"Or maybe you arranged to buy the land illegally," he said, "and you're responsible for murder."

"How dare you?" She raised her hand back, balled it into a fist, tempted to slug him, but his eyebrow went up in challenge, and her sanity returned. She had to get a grip. She couldn't attack the law or she'd end up in jail. Then what would her father do?

"How dare I what?" he asked. "Try to find out the truth? Try to solve the murders that occurred on your property?"

He inched closer, so close his breath brushed her cheek. A breath that hinted at coffee and intimacy and…sex.

She folded her arms, ignoring any temptation to take another whiff. "I thought Billy Whitley killed Marcie James, Daniel Taabe, and those others?"

He shrugged. "We have reason to believe that someone else might be responsible, that Billy Whitley's suicide note might have been forged."

"What makes you think that?"

"The handwriting analysis didn't pan out after all, and the blood used in the ritualistic burial doesn't match Billy's."

"What blood?" Jessie asked.

"The Comanches bury their dead in a ritualistic style. They bend the person's knees, bind them with a rope, then bathe them. Then they paint the deceased's face red, and seal the eyes with clay. The red face paint is made from powdered ochre mixed with fish oil or animal grease and blood." He paused again to make his point. "*Human* blood."

In spite of her bravado, Jessie shivered slightly.

"After that, they dress the deceased in the finest clothing, lay them on a blanket, then wrap the body in another blanket and tie them with buffalo-hide rope. The body is placed in a sitting position on a horse and taken to the burial place west of the Comanche settlement and buried."

"So you really think this land is sacred?"

He gave a clipped nod. "Yes. The cadaver found was definitely Native American, the bones years old."

Jessie rubbed her arms with her hands. "But why would Billy admit that he killed Marcie and Daniel if he didn't?"

Sergeant Navarro's eyes darkened. "Because someone forced him to write that confession, or forged it."

Tension stretched between them as she contemplated his suggestion. "If you think my father did all that, you're crazy."

His jaw tightened. "Your father had means, motive

and opportunity." He gestured toward the crime scenes where the bodies had been discovered, then to the latest grave where the Native American had been uncovered. "But if he's not guilty, then someone else is, and I intend to find them and make them pay."

His big body suddenly stilled, went rigid, his eyes sharp as he turned and scanned the grounds. She saw the animal prints in the soil just as he did. Coyote prints.

He moved forward stealthily like a hunter stalking his prey, tracking the prints. His thick thighs flexed as he climbed over scrub brush and rocks until he reached a copse of oaks and hackberries. Tilting his hat back slightly for a better view, he dropped to his haunches and pawed through the brush.

She hiked over to see what he was looking at. Hopefully not another body. "What is it?"

He held up a small leather pouch he'd hooked by a gloved thumb. "It looks like a woman's."

She knelt beside him to examine it closer, focusing on the beaded flowers on the leather.

"Have you seen it before?" he asked.

He turned it over, revealing the letters *LL* engraved on the other side, and perspiration dampened her breasts. "Yes."

"Whom does it belong to?"

She bit her lip, a memory suffusing her. "LL stands for Linda Lantz. She worked for us as a horse groom a couple of years ago."

He narrowed his eyes. "Where is she now?"

"I don't know. She left the ranch about the same time Marcie was killed."

The Ranger cleared his throat. "And you're just telling us about this now?"

She jutted up her chin defiantly. "I didn't think her leaving had anything to do with Marcie's disappearance and death. Linda had been talking about moving closer to her family in Wyoming so I assumed she left to go home."

"Without giving you notice?"

She shrugged. "It happens."

"Well, if she left that long ago, then this pouch has been here for two years. That makes her a possible suspect..." He let the sentence trail off and Jessie filled in the blanks.

A suspect or perhaps another victim.

Worried, she stood, massaging her temple as she tried to remember if Linda had acted oddly those last few weeks.

"Did she know Marcie?" Ranger Navarro asked.

"I don't think so, but they could have met in town."

He cleared his throat. "Maybe she disappeared because she knows something about the murders. What if she stumbled on the killer burying the bodies out here?"

"Oh, God..." Jessie sighed. "I hope that's not true. Linda was a nice girl."

A heartbeat of silence ticked between them. That knot of anxiety in her stomach gnawed deeper. What if Linda's body was buried here, too? What if it had been here for two years? Maybe she should have reported her missing.

The sound of animals scurrying in the distance reverberated through the hackberries and mesquites, then a menacing growl—a coyote?

Odd. Coyotes usually surfaced at night, not morning.

"They're watching," he said in a low tone.

"What?" Jessie searched the early morning shadows dancing through the trees. "Who's watching?"

"The spirits of the dead," he said in a quiet tone, as if he could see them. "Their sacred burial ground has been disturbed, one of their own moved, and they want the body returned."

Jessie tipped back the brim of her hat and studied him. "You really believe that?"

He nodded matter-of-factly. "See that tzensa on the ridge."

"That what?"

"Coyote."

"Yes." Intrigued that a man of the law believed in folk legends, she followed him as he walked over to a cluster of rocks, then peered up toward the ridge at the coyote as if he was silently communicating with it.

"The tzensa is an omen that something unpleasant is going to happen," he said in a deep, almost hypnotic tone. "He may even be a skin walker."

In spite of the warm spring sunshine, a chill skated up Jessie's arms. He'd followed the coyote's prints to the leather pouch. "What exactly is a skin walker?"

He gave her a questioning look as if he suspected her to make fun of him, then must have decided that either she wasn't, or that he didn't care and continued. "According to the Comanches, when an evil spirit is angered, it wants revenge and can sometimes possess the body of an animal."

Jessie shook her head. "That's a little far-fetched, isn't it?"

He gave a sardonic chuckle. "Some would say the same about religion."

Jessie mentally conceded the point. "You're a Ranger. I thought you believed in forensics and cold, hard evidence, not in superstitions."

He lifted his head as if he smelled something in the air, something unpleasant. Maybe dangerous. "A good cop uses both the physical evidence and his instincts."

She sighed, hands on her hips. "This is unreal. First you accuse my family of stealing land, then murder. And now you expect me to believe that evil spirits are here, wanting revenge."

His dark eyes fastened on her, unnerving and deadly serious. "Your father disturbed them when he bought the sacred land, and then that road crew stirred them up even more."

"If the land is indeed sacred, we had no idea when we closed the deal," Jessie argued. "And I sure as heck didn't expect anyone to be killed over it."

"But your father set the chain of events into motion," the Ranger said. "And now, if I'm right, you and your father may be in danger from the spirits."

"I'm not worried about spirits." Jessie waved her hand in a dismissive gesture. "But go ahead and do your job, Ranger. The sooner you arrest the real killer, the sooner you can leave us alone, and our lives can return to normal."

His gaze met hers, determination flashing in his steely gaze, but a warning also darkened the depths. She barely resisted another shiver. He really believed those legends.

But she was a by-the-book kind of girl. The danger lay in the Native American activists threatening her family, and the killer whom the Rangers obviously hadn't yet arrested.

Not some angered spirits.

Still, as if to defy her, the coyote suddenly howled from the top of the ridge and a gust of wind rustled the trees, the scent of the death on her land surrounding her.

CABE SILENTLY CURSED.

Hell, he knew how people in the town looked down upon the Native legends. But for a moment, something crazy had possessed him, and he'd spilled his guts to Jessie.

A mistake he wouldn't do again. She was the enemy. He was supposed to extract information from her, not the other way around.

But as much as he'd left the old ways and superstitions behind, he couldn't ignore his instincts. He felt the evil spirit lingering as he stared into the tzensa's eyes. The coyote was a great predator, a trickster.

And he was here for a reason. Cabe had felt the connection.

The animal angled its mangy head toward the ridge below as if silently passing on a message, and Cabe headed toward the spot where the tzensa had looked. Sun glinted off rocks and what looked like a bat cave below, and he skidded down the hill, climbing over shrubs and sagebrush, dirt and crumbled stones skidding beneath his rawhide boots.

Behind him, Jessie followed, her soft breaths puffing

out as she descended the hill. He spotted the dark entrance to the bat cave nearby. Weeds and brush shadowed the opening, and he frowned, grateful that bats were nocturnal and he didn't have to face them now. At night they'd be swarming.

He rounded a big boulder, and came to an abrupt halt. Owl feathers.

An owl was a sign of death.

The ground had been disturbed, clawed away, the earth upturned. He gritted his teeth, then dropped to his haunches and studied the claw marks. The tzensa's…

Bones poked through the soil, and a dirt-crusted silver headdress with emeralds embedded in the Native etchings shimmered in the sunlight.

"What did you find now?" Jessie asked behind him.

He shifted slightly as she approached so she could see for herself.

"Oh, my God," Jessie gasped as she spotted the skeleton.

A rustling sound followed, and Cabe jerked his head toward the woods, his heart pounding as he spotted a shadow floating between the oaks. Someone was there, watching them.

Someone who posed a danger.

A second later, a gunshot pinged off the boulder beside them. Jessie screamed.

He shoved her down to the ground, grabbed his gun and tried to shield her as another bullet flew toward them.

Chapter Two

Jessie's knees slammed into the ground as the Ranger threw her down and covered her with his body. Hard muscle pressed against her, his breath heaving into her ear, his shoulder pressing hers into the ground, his legs trapping her.

The scent of man and sweat assaulted her, then she tasted dirt. Pinned down by his big body, a panicky feeling seized her, and she pushed against him to escape. But another bullet zoomed within inches of them, bouncing off the boulder, and he rolled her sideways until they were near the bat cave, and hidden by the thorny brush.

"Stay down!" he growled in her ear.

Jessie heaved a breath, wishing she had the gun in her saddlebag. "Do you see the shooter?"

The Ranger lifted his head, bracing his Sig Sauer to fire as he scanned the horizon. She raised her head as well, searching and struggling to crawl out from under him. The big damn man was smothering her.

He jerked his head toward his SUV. "Get in my Land Rover, lock the doors and stay down. I'm going after him."

Without waiting on her reply, he jumped up, ducking behind brush and trees as he ran toward her horse, vaulted onto it and sent the palomino into a gallop toward the woods where the shots had come from.

"No!" She launched after him. No one rode Firebird but *her.* The nerve of the arrogant bastard. This was her land—she had to protect it.

But she wasn't a fool either. He had just ridden off with her weapon and she couldn't chase the shooter on foot.

Another shot skidded by her ear, nearly clipping her, and she realized she had no choice. It was the bat cave or his Land Rover, and she didn't intend to tangle with the bats.

She crouched low and sprinted toward his Land Rover, furious, and hoping he caught the man.

Firebird's hooves pounded the ground, and the shots faded as she climbed in the Land Rover, locked the doors and crouched on the seat. Tension thrummed through her body as she waited and listened. She felt like a sitting duck and lifted her head just enough to peer out the window to watch in case the shooter snuck up on her.

Her temper flaring, she checked for the keys to the vehicle. She'd drive it back to the house and leave the surly Ranger just as he had left her. But of course, the keys were missing.

Probably in his damn pocket.

Steaming with anger, she folded her arms and tapped her snakeskin boots on the floor while she waited.

Ever since her father had purchased that land, their lives had fallen apart.

When they'd first discussed the deal, he'd been

excited about the prospects of expanding his operations. She'd still been in college, but she'd grown tired of following her mother around from one man to another. So, she'd finished her degree and decided to come back to the ranch, reunite with her father and join his operation.

But when she'd returned, she'd immediately sensed something was wrong with him. Although the cattle operation was successful, her father had made some other poor investments. Odd, since he was usually such a shrewd businessman.

After reviewing the books, she'd realized they had to increase their cash flow, so she'd added boarding and training quarter horses to the cattle operation. With even bigger ranches than the Becker one around needing working horses, she'd struck a deal to train them and had increased their cash flow within months, enabling him to pay off the debts he'd accrued and steer the ranch back on track.

But her father's behavior had worried her.

At first, she couldn't pinpoint what was wrong, but little things had seemed out of sync, and she feared his memory had been slipping. He'd complained of seeing things on the land, of hearing voices and bad things happening. Lights flickering on and off. Shadows in the house. Cattle missing. A watering hole that had dried up when they had had torrential rains. Fences broken. A small barn fire that had nearly spread out of control which could have been dangerous for the livestock and ranch hands.

And now these murders.

Sergeant Navarro's warning about danger from the

spirits taunted her, but she blew it off. Spirits didn't fire guns or start fires.

Whoever had killed Marcie and the others was obviously still lurking around. And they didn't want her or the Rangers asking questions.

CABE KICKED THE PALOMINO'S sides and they galloped up the hill, scouring the wooded area where the shooter had disappeared. Another bullet soared near his head, and he ducked, then fired off a round with his Sig Sauer. The horse protested, whinnying and backing up, but he gave the animal a swift kick to urge him forward.

Another shot whizzed by his shoulder, and Cabe cursed and coaxed the horse around another bend of trees, but the shadow was gone, and the trees were too thick to maneuver the horse through, so he brought the animal to a stop, jumped off and ran into the copse of oaks.

He spotted a shadow moving ahead—the tzensa— then jogged to the east where the road lay, in case the shooter had a car ahead. Another bullet pinged off the oak beside him, the bushes to his right rustling as the man dashed through them. Cabe raced toward him, but a rattler suddenly lurched from the bushes in attack.

"Easy," he said in a low voice. Not wanting to kill the diamondback, he froze, aware any sudden movement would bring it hissing at him.

In the distance, an engine roared to life. He cursed. He was losing the shooter.

Furious, he grabbed a stick, picked the snake up and whirled it away, then jogged toward the sound of the car. The wind ruffled the mesquite as he made it to the clearing. The creek gurgled, water rippling over jagged rocks, and a vulture soared above, its squawk breaking the silence.

But the car disappeared into a cloud of dust so thick that Cabe couldn't detect the make of the vehicle or see a license plate. Dammit.

He'd never catch the car on foot, or horseback for that matter.

Stowing his gun in his holster, he turned and sprinted back to where he'd left the palomino, climbed on it, then rode back to the crime scene. He had to protect the evidence. Then there was the problem of Jessie Becker.

Mentally, he stewed over the identity of the shooter, considering their current suspects. Her father for one.

Jonah Becker was a ruthless businessman, but to chance hurting his own daughter—would he stoop that low?

The sun was rising higher in the midmorning sky and blazing hotter by the time he reached the crime scene, his senses honed. What if the shooter had been a distraction to mess with the crime scene? What if he'd had an accomplice and he'd gotten to Jessie Becker?

Slowing the palomino as he approached, he scanned the area. The original graves that had held the body of the antiquities broker and activist were still roped off with crime scene tape. Still keeping his gun at the ready, he dismounted, then checked the gravesites to verify that nothing had been disturbed. Everything appeared to be intact.

In two quick strides, he reached his crime kit, and examined it to verify that the evidence he'd collected was still inside. A lawyer could argue that it had been left, unguarded, and could have been compromised.

Hell. He didn't want to lose the case on a technicality.

Maybe Jessie could tell him if she'd seen anyone else around.

Sweat beaded on his neck as he strode over to his Land Rover. But when he reached for the door handle and looked inside, Jessie was gone.

His heart stuttered in his chest. God, he hoped there hadn't been another shooter.

He didn't want anyone dying on his watch. Even Jessie.

JESSE LAUNCHED HERSELF AT the Ranger and shoved him up against the Land Rover. "What in the hell were you were doing taking my horse and leaving me unarmed?"

A shocked look crossed his face, then fury flashed into his eyes, and he grabbed her arms to fend off her attack. "Trying to save your pretty little ass," he barked. "And why didn't you stay in the car like I ordered?"

"Because I don't take orders from anyone." Her pulse clamored, a mixture of anger at him mingling with relief that he'd returned and the shooter was gone. Although she'd never admit that to him. Then his comment registered, and she couldn't resist taunting him. "So you think my ass is pretty?"

His jaw tightened as if he was working to control his temper, and regretted any compliment, no matter how backhanded it was. "You have a gun?"

Good grief, he was going to turn the tables on her. "Of course. I live on a ranch, Sergeant. I have to protect myself from snakes and rustlers and whatever else." She gave him a challenging look. "And before you ask, yes, I know how to use it."

His eyebrow lift infuriated her more. "You're surprised? Don't tell me you were expecting some spoiled, rich girl with a dozen servants who lives off her daddy's dime."

His evil smile confirmed she'd hit the nail on the head.

She huffed in disgust. "For your information, I have a master's in business administration," she continued, squaring her shoulders. "I started the quarter horse training operation, and now we supply working horses to other ranchers. And I not only run the books, but work the ranch myself. I'm a damn good horse trainer, if I do say so myself."

"I bet you are," he said with a sultry smile that made her belly clench.

For a moment the air changed between them, their eyes locked, and she sensed she'd won his admiration.

Then his frown returned, and he gestured toward the spot where they'd found the bones. "Then you oversaw the purchase of this land?"

She stiffened, knowing he was backing her into a corner and yanked away from his grip. In spite of his razor-sharp voice, his touch had been protective and almost…tender.

She couldn't let him confuse her with those touches, or seduce her into incriminating her family. She was *not* her mother, a woman who fell into bed with every man who looked at her.

"No," she said cautiously, back in control. "Dad made the deal when I was away at school finishing my degree."

"How about your brother, Trace?"

She bit her lip. Things had been tense between her and Trace since she'd moved back. Because of Trace's animosity, she was staying in one of the small cabins on the property instead of the main house. "He put the deal together," she admitted.

"And your father's lawyer, Jerry Collier, handled the sale?"

She nodded.

"I'll need to question your father, brother and Collier."

That knot of worry in her stomach grew exponentially. She only prayed her father handled the interview without looking incompetent—or guilty. Between his ruthless business tactics, and his recent memory lapses, he might just hang himself.

"You're going to talk to them now?" she asked.

He regarded her with suspicion in his eyes. "No, but soon. First I have to take care of business, obtain that injunction against this land being used until the land issue is resolved and transport the evidence I collected to trace." He heaved a breath. "Did you see anyone else here after I rode off?"

"No."

"No one could have touched my crime kit?"

She narrowed her eyes as if she realized the direction of his thoughts. "No, there was no one else here. And I didn't touch your kit or the evidence."

"How do I know I can trust you? You and I don't exactly have the same agenda."

His husky voice skated over her with distrust…and sexual innuendo. Damn, the man was so seductive that for a moment, her chest pounded, and she wanted to win his trust. But she would not allow him to turn her into a pile of feminine mush.

"Yes, I want to clear my family's name," she said, "but I also know that the best way to do that is for you to find the truth."

Another long, intense look, and she barely resisted the urge to fidget—or turn tail and run. Normally his size and stare probably intimidated men and women, but she refused to allow him to rattle her. She lived in a man's world, did jobs men did on the ranch.

"You can take my prints if you want," she said with a saccharine smile.

A deep chuckle rumbled from within him. "If the lab turns up prints, I will."

She planted her hands on her hips. "So, what now, Sergeant?"

She intentionally made his title sound like a four-letter word, and was rewarded when a muscle ticked in his jaw.

"I'm going to look for the bullets and casings from the shooter, then make sure this crime scene and those burial sites are guarded around the clock."

She frowned, half wanting to stick around to see what else he discovered—and to watch him work. But she needed to check on her father and warn him about the Ranger. Hopefully her dad and Trace both had alibis for this morning. Her father had still been in bed when she'd stopped by for coffee, but Trace had already left the house. He was somewhere on the ranch.

He'd been adamant about getting rid of the Rangers. Would he have shot at this one to try to run him off?

Irritated, she turned and headed toward Firebird, but the Ranger called her name, his voice taunting.

"Where are you going, Jessie? Running to warn Daddy that I found more damning evidence against him? That I intend to take a sample of his blood to see if it matches the red paint used in the ritualistic burials so I can nail him for murder?"

She schooled her reaction, then offered him a sardonic look. "No, Sergeant. My father is innocent. Get a warrant and take your blood sample, and *you'll* prove it." She swung up into the saddle and glared down at him again. "And in spite of the fact that you're trying to take away our land and destroy our reputation, I have a ranch to run."

The challenge in his dark eyes sent her stomach fluttering again, then his look softened, turned almost concerned. "Be careful, Jessie," he finally said in a gruff voice. "Remember there's a shooter out there, and he may still be on your property."

She patted her saddlebag where she kept her pistol. "Don't worry. I can take care of myself." Settling her hat more firmly on her head, she clicked her heels against the mare's flanks, yanked the reins and sent Firebird galloping toward the main ranch house.

But his warning reverberated in her head, and she kept her eyes peeled as she crossed the distance in case the shooter was still lurking around. Not only were the Native Americans incensed about the land deal, but other locals were jealous of her father's success.

One of them had shot at the Ranger and her today.

She didn't intend to end up dead like the others.

A TIGHTNESS GRIPPED CABE'S chest as he watched Jessie disappear into the distance.

She was undeniably the most stubborn, independent, infuriating, spunky, sexy woman he'd ever met.

Even when she'd been hissing at him like a rattlesnake, his body had hummed to life with arousal. Unfortunately, the fact that she was so devoted to her family and defended her father to no end only stirred his admiration.

And she could tame a wild horse. Damn he was sure of that. In fact, he'd like to climb in the saddle with her and tangle a time or two.

He almost hated to take down her father and destroy her image of him. Or cause her any grief.

But the wind whispered with the scent of death, the murder victims' faces swam in his mind, the Native spirits screaming for justice.

He'd do whatever was necessary to ferret out the truth.

Jonah Becker and his son, Trace, had no scruples—that was the key to their success. Was it the key to Jessie's rise in the ranching business as well? Was she really going back to work, or running to help her father cover his crimes?

Remembering the hairs he'd found, the clay sample and the leather pouch, he punched in Lt. Wyatt Colter's number. Wyatt had been the first Ranger working the case and the lead. "Navarro."

Wyatt cleared his throat. "Yeah?"

Cabe explained about the evidence he'd collected and the attack.

"If someone forged Billy's suicide note or forced him to write it, then killed him," Wyatt said, "they obviously don't want us still poking around."

"Which means that Billy may not have killed the antiquities dealer, the activist, Marcie or Daniel Taabe. So the real killer is still at large and definitely wanted to scare me off."

"Maybe it was Jonah Becker or his son," Wyatt suggested. "We still believe he obtained that land illegally."

"Could have been one of them, I guess, but Jessie Becker was with me. She could have been hit as well."

"Dammit, this case has been nothing but trouble. Someone's been tampering with the evidence every step of the way." A long, tense moment passed. "Keep the scene secure and make sure you follow the chain of custody. When we catch this bastard, we don't want him to walk."

Cabe bit back a sarcastic remark. "I know how to do my job, Lieutenant. I'll take the evidence to the sheriff's office and have a Ranger courier pick it up to transport to the lab. But first, I'm going to search for the bullets and casings from the shooter." A noise in the brush drew his eyes, and he turned to study the woods again, wondering if the killer had returned.

"I also found a leather pouch with the initials *LL* on it. Jessie said it belonged to a horse groom named Linda Lantz who worked for her two years ago. Apparently Linda left the ranch about the same time Marcie faked her kidnapping and death."

"So she might have been involved?" Wyatt asked.

"Or she could be a witness. We need to find out if she's still alive. And if so, where she is now."

Wyatt mumbled agreement. "I'll see what I can dig up on her."

Cabe cleared his throat. "One more thing. I discovered another burial spot. I'm sure this one is an old grave, a Native American female, but I'll need the ME and Dr. Jacobsen for verification."

"We should excavate the entire area," Wyatt suggested.

"No," Cabe said emphatically. "These last two bodies suggest that this is definitely a sacred burial ground. We can't remove bodies or disturb the dead."

"But—"

"I'm telling you we can't," Cabe said sharply. "Besides the legal problems, it's too dangerous, Wyatt. The dead are already incensed over what's been done to them here. If we start digging up the bodies and moving them, the spirits will be even more angry and dangerous."

"You really believe in all this superstition?"

Cabe chewed the inside of his cheek. He'd hated the traditions, the way some of the Natives on the reservation refused to acclimate with the rest of the modern world. The animosity between the two sects in town and the old prejudices that refused to die.

But he couldn't deny some of the things he'd seen and experienced growing up. And again today.

"Yes," Cabe said. "And if you think the Native American faction in Comanche Creek is up in arms now, just try to dig up a sacred burial ground."

Wyatt sighed. "So what do you suggest we do?"

"Inform the forensic anthropologist that we have to do everything we can to preserve the burial grounds, any artifacts here, and identify the bones."

"Don't worry. Nina would do that anyway. She's very protective of her finds."

"Good." Cabe scrubbed his hand over the back of his neck. "I'm going to call a meeting of the Town Council and the leaders of the Native American faction. A court injunction should stop any more use of the land by the Beckers until the matter is resolved. Hopefully that will soothe ruffled feathers long enough for us to sort things out and find our murderer."

"I'll arrange for Deputy Spears and some floating deputies to guard the land twenty-four seven," Wyatt said. "Even though Deputy Shane Tolbert was cleared, I don't want him near our crime scene. His past relationship with Marcie still poses a conflict of interest."

"He strikes me as a hothead," Cabe said.

"He is," Wyatt agreed. "What about the Becker family?"

Cabe shifted and scrubbed dirt from his boots. "I'll question Jonah and his son and get a warrant for blood samples from both of them. If one of their blood matches the paint from Daniel Taabe's body, we'll know who's to blame."

"What about the daughter? Do you think she's covering for her father?"

Cabe hesitated. He wanted to believe that Jessie was innocent. But he'd hold off judgment until he fished around some more. "I don't know yet, but I'll keep an eye on her."

For some reason, the thought of spying on her disturbed him.

And she'd felt downright sinful when he'd covered her body with his. Of course, she'd shoved at him to get off her. She'd obviously hated him touching her.

Yep. Jessie Becker was a hands-off case.

He absolutely couldn't get involved with her. She and her family were his prime suspects.

And if she was covering for her father, he'd have to throw the book at her as an accessory.

Chapter Three

Jessie frowned as she rode back to the main house. If Billy Whitley hadn't killed Marcie and the others, then who had?

Deputy Shane Tolbert's father, Ben? He'd confessed to shooting at Sergeant Hutton and the sheriff, but he denied killing Billy, Marcie, Daniel Taabe, the antiquities broker and the Native American activist who first accused Jonah of the illegal land deal.

Instead of the investigation coming to an end, the situation was growing worse. The Rangers had only allowed her on their task force because she knew the lay of the land, and they trusted her more than they did her father or brother.

Then again, they had probably asked her to join them so they could watch her as a suspect.

Jessie tied the palomino to the hitching post, the sight of the Bluebonnets and Indian paintbrushes swaying in the breeze.

Spring was usually her favorite time of year, a time where life was renewed, the land blossomed with an array of colors, green leaves and flowers, and the beautiful blue of the Texas sky turned glorious shades as winter's gray faded and the sun glinted off the rugged land.

She paused to inhale the scent of fresh grass filling the air, but the memory of the brittle skeleton bones she'd seen haunted her—instead of life thriving now, there was too much death on their land. Violence and suspicion had invaded her home like a dark cloud.

She stomped up the steps to the porch, determined to protect her own. The ranch and her father were her life. And now that life and her family's future and good name were in jeopardy.

Her head ached from anxiety, and her shoulders were knotted and sore. She shoved open the door to the scent of freshly baked cinnamon bread, coffee and bacon, but her stomach churned. She couldn't eat a bite.

Lolita, the cook who had been with her father for years, loped in with a smile. "You hungry, Miss Jessie?"

She shook her head. "No, thanks. Is Dad downstairs yet?"

Lolita gave a short nod, but concern darkened her brown eyes. "In his private study. I took him coffee, and he's resting in his easy chair."

Good, at least he had an alibi. Not that Lolita wouldn't lie for him, but Jessie hoped to clear the family with the truth. "Did he have a hard night?"

Lolita nodded. "I heard him pacing the floor until near dawn."

"I'll check on him now." She swung around to the right, then knocked on her father's study door. He had insisted on maintaining a small private space for himself, so she and Trace shared a connecting office next door.

Expensive, dark leather furniture and a bulky credenza gave the room a masculine feel. An ornately carved wooden box sat on his desk where he kept his pipe tobacco, and built-in paneled bookcases held his collection of leather-bound historical journals and books.

A portrait of his father, William Becker, hung above the brick mantel, a testament to the man who'd bought the small parcel of land that had been the beginnings of the Becker ranch. He'd named it the Big B because of his drive to make it one of the biggest spreads in Texas, and first brought in the Santa Gertrudis which they still raised.

Her father didn't answer, so she knocked again, then cracked the door open. "Dad?"

He glanced up from his newspaper, took a sip of his coffee, his brows furrowed. "Jessie?"

She breathed a sigh of relief that he recognized her. Twice lately, he'd called her by her mother's name. She'd think he was still grieving for her, but they'd divorced years ago. "Yes. We need to talk."

He twisted the left side of his handlebar mustache, a familiar habit. "Come on in."

She moved into the room and settled on the leather love seat across from him. "Dad, another Ranger was here today, a Native American named Sergeant Cabe Navarro."

Worry knitted his brows together, and he tapped his pipe and lit it. "They brought in an Indian."

Jessie worked her mouth from side to side. "Yes, he's a Comanche, and you should show him some respect. Besides, this one is a Texas Ranger. He's sworn to uphold the law." And he'd probably had to overcome severe obstacles and prejudices to achieve his goals.

That realization roused admiration in her chest.

"Those Rangers need to leave us alone," her father spat.

"I know it upsets you, Dad, but they're not leaving until these murders have been solved and the issue of the land is resolved."

"Hell, I thought Billy Whitley admitted to the murders before he killed himself."

"The Rangers think the suicide/confession note might have been bogus, that someone might have forced Billy to write it, or that it was forged."

"Good God Almighty." Her father coughed and leaned back in his chair, looking pale and weak. "So what does that mean?"

"That Billy may have possessed evidence proving he doctored that paperwork on the land deal." Which meant the Native Americans were right. They deserved the land, and her father had made an illegal deal.

Protective instincts swelled inside her, and she clenched her teeth. He was a ruthless businessman, but he wouldn't have knowingly agreed to an illegal deal, would he?

No… He'd been acting oddly lately, not himself, his memory slipping. He'd undergone every test imaginable since her return, and the doctors could prove nothing. So why was her father's health deteriorating?

She might suspect guilt or grief was eating at him, but she didn't believe him capable of murder. And grief for strangers was not something he would feel. He'd hardened himself against loving anyone, had shut himself off from friendships and close relationships after her mother had run off with a ranch hand. Instead, he'd focused all his attention on building his business empire.

"Dad, there's more," Jessie said softly. "Ranger Navarro discovered another body today, a Native American he believes was buried years ago." She reached out and touched his hand. "Be honest with me, Dad. Did you know the property was a sacred burial ground when you bought it?"

"Don't be ridiculous," her father said, the strength in his voice reminding her of her old father, not the frail man he'd been lately, the man she'd feared might be suffering from early-onset Alzheimer's or dementia.

The man she tried to hide from the press and police.

If word leaked that Jonah Becker was seriously ill, especially mentally incapacitated, not only would the cops attack, so would the media and his competitors. Jonah's business investors might also lose faith in him and drop their support.

"They can't do that to us." Her father slapped a shaky hand on the arm of his chair.

"Dad, the land is the least of our worries," Jessie said. Not that she wanted her father arrested for a fraudulent deal, but murder was much more serious. "Daniel Taabe's body was buried in a Comanche ritualistic style just as those other two were. The face was painted with red paint, paint which has human blood in it. The blood didn't match Billy Whitley's, so now the Rangers believe that Billy didn't kill Marcie and Daniel, that someone forced him to confess to their murders, then killed him."

"I don't understand." That confused look she'd seen

the past weeks momentarily glazed his eyes. Releasing a weary sigh, he puffed on his pipe. A moment passed, then his lucidity returned.

"Someone else in this town killed them," her father snapped. "A lot of people in Comanche Creek are jealous of us, Jessie. Jealous of me and my success." He turned toward her, his eyes imploring. "Don't you see? Someone is trying to frame me."

Jessie squeezed her hand over her father's. "You're probably right," she said with an encouraging smile. "I'll find out who's doing this, I promise, Daddy."

Suddenly the door burst open, and her brother, Trace, stormed in. "What in the hell is going on, Jessie?"

She stiffened. "Calm down, Trace. What's wrong?"

"I heard you were hanging out with that Comanche Ranger. What were you doing, trying to help him hang us out to dry?"

Hurt mushroomed in Jessie's chest. Her brother had resented their mother for taking Jessie with her when she'd left and for leaving him behind. He also resented her return and any attention her father gave her now. He even hated the fact that the horse training she had arranged had garnered success.

And he looked sweaty and winded, panic in his eyes. Suspicions mounted in Jessie's mind. Trace had arranged the deal with Jerry Collier, and would do anything to win his father's favor and safeguard the family ranch.

She flinched, hating her own train of thought. Had Trace known the land was an ancient burial ground, that the papers giving ownership to their father had been doctored?

A sick feeling gnawed at her at the venom in his eyes. Had he killed Daniel or Marcie to keep his secrets and protect the business?

Was he the shooter who'd fired at her and the Ranger a few minutes ago and tried to kill them?

CABE PAWED THROUGH THE brush and dirt, examining trees and rocks for the bullets and casings. After several minutes, he finally located two bullets, one embedded in a shattered tree limb on the ground near where they'd crouched in hiding, the second a partial one that had hit the boulder, warped and landed on the ground a few feet from the grave he'd just discovered.

He searched for footprints, and noticed matted grass, but there were no definitive footprints, nothing clear enough to make a plaster cast.

A mud-splattered vehicle pulled up, gears grinding as it slowed to a stop. Dr. Nina Jacobsen, the forensic anthropologist who'd worked the original crime scene with Wyatt, threw her hand up in greeting as she climbed out.

He'd heard she and the lieutenant had hooked up during the investigation—like Sheriff Hardin and Livvy—and that they planned to marry.

"Wyatt said you found another body," Nina said as she approached.

"Yeah," Cabe said. "Evidence suggests it's a Native American female."

A smile of excitement tilted her mouth. "Then I was right. I thought this property was sacred."

The energy of the spirits and the sound of their cries reverberated through the air, and Cabe nodded, then led her down the embankment around the boulder to point out the latest find. "Wyatt is working on a court injunction to prevent the land from being touched and the bodies moved," Cabe said. "But we have to verify that the bones are not a recent murder, and if possible, identify who they belong to."

Nina squinted through the sunlight, excitement lighting her face as she skidded across the rocky terrain, and halted to hover over the bones. "Judging from that headdress, which looks like it might have been from the 1700s, you're probably right about it being a female. But I'll need to study the bones in detail to verify the age and sex."

"As long as you don't move the body," Cabe said.

"I understand." Nina's ponytail bobbed as she nodded. "Wyatt also mentioned that you found a leather pouch."

"Yeah, Jessie Becker identified it as belonging to one of her groomsmen who worked here two years ago, a woman named Linda Lantz. Let's just hope the girl it belonged to isn't dead and buried on the property as well."

Another vehicle rolled up the drive, this one a squad car.

"That's Deputy Spears," Nina said, shading her eyes with her hand. "He's been taking shifts guarding the site with the floating deputies Sheriff Hardin called in."

"Good. Once the Native Americans hear we found another Native buried here, some of them may be tempted to come out to pray for the dead."

"Or protest," Nina said. "That woman Ellie Penateka has been leading marches at the county office for months."

Ellie—a name blasted from the past. "I know. And I don't want trouble out here."

Nina adjusted her camera over her shoulder. "Don't worry. I'll alert you if there's a problem. I want to preserve and document this find myself."

A blond deputy climbed out and strode toward them, his stance wary as he studied Cabe. "Deputy Spears. Sheriff Hardin sent me."

Cabe shook his hand and introduced himself.

"I heard there was a shooting," Spears said. "Is Jessie all right?"

Something about his tone sounded personal. "She's fine," Cabe said. "Are you two…involved?"

A faint blush crept on the young man's face suggesting he wanted to be. "No. Not really. But I was worried about her."

Cabe clenched his jaw. What did it matter if the deputy and Jessie hooked up? Once this case was over, he'd be hauling ass out of Comanche Creek.

"I'm going to run some evidence by the sheriff's office, then call a meeting of the town and local Native American faction to update them on the investigation."

Spears nodded. "Don't worry. I'll guard the area."

Yeah, and he'd probably guard Jessie if the need arose. But Cabe would handle Jessie himself. He didn't trust anyone else.

"Good luck," Nina said, as she headed back to her SUV to grab her equipment.

Cabe stowed the bagged bullets he'd recovered in his evidence kit, then started the engine, hit the gas and sped toward the road leading into town.

A few minutes later, he dropped the evidence at the sheriff's office, signed the chain of custody form for the courier, then phoned Mayor Sadler to request a town meeting. Sadler agreed to call the Town Council as well as the leaders of the Native American faction.

Cabe grabbed a quick bite at the diner, then headed back to the inn, showered and shaved. With an hour to kill before the meeting, he jotted down notes on the case and his discoveries.

At seven o'clock, he strode over to the town hall, his senses honed for trouble as he watched several people entering the building. Voices drifted to him from the meeting room, and when he went inside, the room was packed with a mixture of Native Americans, Hispanics and Caucasians.

A rugged-looking man with salt-and-pepper hair lumbered up to him and extended his hand. "I'm Mayor Woody Sadler."

So this was the man who'd raised Sheriff Reed Hardin. He'd also been spotted at the cabin where Marcie had been murdered, making him a suspect as well. Although Sheriff Hardin staunchly defended the man's innocence.

Cabe shook Sadler's hand. "Sergeant Navarro."

"Glad you're here," the mayor said. "Maybe you can calm these Indians down."

Anger churned in Cabe's gut. "There are two sides to every argument, Sadler, and I'm not here to play favorites, just to uncover the truth."

Sadler's bushy eyebrows rose with distress, sweat beading on his forehead. "Don't forget, Sergeant. This is my town, and if you make things worse, then you won't last long."

Cabe shot him a challenging look. "Is that a threat, Mayor?"

A smile suddenly stretched the man's weathered face. "Of course not, Sergeant. I'm sure you'll do the right thing."

"I'll do the *honest* thing," Cabe said in a calm but firm voice. "I'll find the killer and the truth about who that land belongs to." He took an intimidating step closer. "And no one will stop me or interfere."

The voices in the room grew heated, cutting into the tension vibrating between Cabe and the mayor. Anger from opposing sides charged the room as hushed mumbles and complaints echoed along the rows of people seated in metal folding chairs.

Cabe frowned at the mayor. "I requested a small meeting with just the leaders. You know this could get out of hand."

Mayor Sadler folded his beefy arms. "This matter concerns everyone in Comanche Creek. And I'm counting on you to keep the situation under control. That is why they sent a Native, isn't it?"

A muscle ticked in Cabe's jaw. "They sent me to bridge the gap." And maybe balance out the underdogs, the Comanches.

Out of the corner of his eye, Cabe spotted the sheriff scrutinizing him. Yes, Hardin definitely was protective of the mayor.

But Wyatt had assured him that Hardin was a professional and had done everything by the book.

Hardin stalked over to him. "I hope you're not going to stir up the town, Navarro."

Cabe's jaw tightened as he repeated his comment to the mayor. "I'm on the side of the law." He tapped the badge on his chest for emphasis.

Hardin gave a clipped nod. "Good. Then let's keep it orderly."

"I'll do my part, and you do yours," Cabe muttered.

The mayor loped over to the podium, and Cabe studied the room. Deputy Shane Tolbert stood leaning against the doorjamb in the back, his arms crossed, his posture antagonistic.

Tolbert had been cleared of Marcie's murder, but he still appeared on the defensive. That fact alone raised Cabe's suspicions. Evidence could be tampered with, doctored, especially by someone with the right knowledge. And Tolbert had taken classes in crime scene investigation.

Plastering on his stony face, he walked to the front to join the mayor, still skimming the crowd. Ellie Penateka waved two fingers at him from the front row. As always, she was dressed to seek attention in tight jeans and a bright red, hand-beaded he was sure, shirt that hugged her big breasts. Her long black hair gleamed beneath the fluorescent light, her brown eyes just as cunning as always. Ellie would use any asset she had to achieve her goal.

At one time, the two of them had been lovers, but she'd wanted, no demanded, more—a commitment. That and for him to join her as an activist for the Native American faction.

He'd said no to both and Ellie hadn't liked it.

Another young woman, this one with black hair tied in a scarf, sat in the second row, fidgeting with the scarf as if to hide her face. She looked nervous, frightened like a skittish colt. Senses alert for trouble, he studied her for a moment, wondering why she refused to make eye contact, and where she stood on the issues in town.

His old friend Rafe Running Horse gave him a friendly nod from a side row, but glares of contempt and distrust followed him as he stepped behind the podium. Jessie Becker's flaming red hair caught in the overhead light, and his gaze locked with hers for a moment, her body language defensive. But he also sensed that she wanted the truth and a peaceful resolution. Or could he be wrong?

Had her family solicited her to wield her feminine seductive powers on him to sidetrack him from arresting them? Hell, if that was the case, it wouldn't work.

Besides, he doubted Jonah Becker would encourage any kind of relationship between him and Jessie. Judging from everything he'd heard, Becker had made no bones about the fact that he believed the Native Americans were a class beneath him.

Defying Becker would be half the fun in proving him wrong. So much fun that for a brief moment, a fantasy flashed in his wicked head. Jessie Becker beneath him. But not in social class. Hell, race and class didn't matter to him.

But he would like the feel of her curves against him, her breasts in his hands, her naked body writhing as he thrust his hard length into her welcoming body.

He blinked, scrubbed his hand over his eyes, forcing the images away. He was at a damn town meeting, couldn't allow himself to be swayed by a pretty girl. Especially Jessie Becker.

When he focused again, Jessie's brother, Trace, stood with arms crossed beside her, his look filled with rage. Trace Becker was short and squatty and made up for his size with his pissy attitude. Cabe read him like a book. Trace wanted an end to this mess, too, and he didn't care if it was peaceful, as long as his family came out unscathed.

Cabe had expected animosity from the group, and it simmered in the air like a brush fire that had been lit and was ready to flame out of control.

Clenching the sides of the podium, he introduced himself, asked for everyone to listen. Intentionally using a calm voice to soothe the noise, he relayed the latest discoveries in the case.

Before he even finished, Ellie shot up from her seat with a clatter. "So that land definitely is a Native American burial ground?"

He slanted her a warning look not to stir trouble. "It appears that way. We'll release further information when our investigation is complete. Please bear with us though, that will take time. And for purposes of finding the truth, we can't reveal all the details until the investigation is concluded. That also means that the property is off-limits, so please don't show up to protest or gawk. If you do, you will be arrested for interfering with a criminal investigation and sent to jail."

Noises of protest rumbled through the room, but he held up a hand and explained about the injunction. "I need everyone to remain calm and trust us to do our jobs." He gestured toward the sheriff. "Sheriff Hardin, the Texas Rangers and our task force are doing everything possible to settle this matter in a speedy manner and to ensure your safety."

"What about our leader, Daniel Taabe?" a dark-skinned elderly woman with twin braids cried. "You're letting them cover up his murder."

"There is no cover-up," Cabe said staunchly. "We will find out who killed Daniel as well as the other victims in the town and see that they are punished. But we need your cooperation. If anyone has information regarding any of the murders, please inform the sheriff or me."

"I thought Billy Whitley killed Marcie, Daniel and those others," a middle-aged man in overalls shouted.

"The evidence is not supporting Billy's confession," Cabe explained.

"You mean Billy might have been framed?" someone else asked.

"Was he murdered?" a little old woman cried.

A teenage Comanche boy vaulted up from his seat, waving his fist. "He should have died if he faked those documents. That land belongs to us."

Cabe threw up his hands to calm the crowd. "As I stated before, everyone needs to be patient, and let us get to the truth."

Trace lurched toward him, shaking his finger. "Just whose side are you on, Ranger?"

"The side of the law and the truth," Cabe said through clenched teeth.

"You should be on our side," one of the Natives said, triggering agreement to rumble through the crowd from the Natives.

Trace turned to the crowd. "Navarro's not on the side

of the law. He's playing both sides." His voice grew louder, accusing. "He can't be trusted!"

Jessie grabbed her brother's arm in an attempt to pull him back to his seat, but Trace shook her off and charged forward. Others stood and began shouting and arguing, but the sheriff raised his pistol and fired at the ceiling.

"Stop it now," Sheriff Hardin shouted. "If anyone can't control themselves, I will arrest them and lock them up myself."

A newfound respect for Hardin filled Cabe, and he exchanged a silent moment of understanding, then two deputies Hardin must have brought in strode through the crowd restoring order and issuing warnings to those whose tempers were spiking out of control.

Finally the room settled down, and everyone slowly dispersed, the deputies corralling them outside and accompanying them to assure that the arguments from opposing sides didn't escalate into physical violence.

Rafe Running Horse wove through the crowd toward him, and Cabe breathed a sigh of relief that he had his old friend's support. Rafe was one of the few people he'd missed from Comanche Creek, a trusted childhood confidant who'd struggled with his own heritage and goals.

But Trace lunged toward Cabe and grabbed his shirt. "It's bad enough you're trying to take our land, but I know you were at the ranch today. Don't you dare use my sister to try to pin a murder rap on my father."

Cabe ripped Trace's hands off him. "Back off, Becker. If you touch me again, I'll arrest you for assaulting an officer."

Jessie raced up, and tugged at Trace's arm again, a

wariness in her eyes. "Come on, Trace. You're just making things worse."

Becker snarled at her, then pushed her out of the way.

Cabe clenched his jaw, then grabbed Trace's arm in a death grip. "Watch it, Becker."

"You're the one who should watch it, Indian."

Anger cut through him. "It's *Ranger* Sergeant Navarro."

Trace's eyes flashed with fury, then he jerked away and spit on Cabe's shoe.

Cabe fisted his hands beside him to keep from pounding the bastard senseless. But the entire town was watching, and he had asked them to show self-control. He had to provide a role model to them now.

"Get out of here, Trace," Sheriff Hardin growled.

Trace laughed bitterly, then spun around and stalked away.

Jessie shook her head. "I'm sorry, Ranger Navarro. He's just upset."

"He's an ass," Cabe said through gritted teeth.

And her brother's behavior only swayed suspicion toward him. But he didn't have to tell Jessie that—she was smart enough to figure it out. "Like I said earlier, Jessie, be careful."

She stared at him for a long moment, some emotion brimming in her translucent eyes, then spun around and walked away. He watched her leave in case Trace confronted her—or maybe he just liked watching that tumbling red hair shimmering down her back.

Ellie sidled up to him, and stroked a finger along his badge. "What was going on with you and Jessie Becker?"

He tensed, almost sympathizing with Jessie. He had the oddest sense that she carried the weight of the world—at least the weight of her family's problems—on her slender shoulders. "Nothing. Her brother is a jerk."

She lifted a dark brow, her tone suspicious. "How do you know her?"

"I don't," he said curtly, refusing to play Ellie's petty jealous games. "I met her today when I was on the property investigating the crime scenes."

She offered him a small smile, her eyelashes fluttering. "I'm glad you're back in town, Cabe. We need you here."

He braced himself for another Ellie confrontation. "I'm here to do a job, Ellie. I'm not staying long."

Her stifling perfume assailed him as she leaned closer to him. "Maybe I can change your mind this time. Why don't we grab a drink and catch up? I'll buy."

Yeah, but the cost would be too great. "That's not going to happen," he said matter-of-factly. "Nothing could keep me in Comanche Creek, Ellie. You understand. *Nothing.*"

Her lips thinned. "You don't know what you're missing. Cabe. We would be good together, and we could do so much for our people."

He ignored her barb. Ellie had her own political aspirations, and would achieve them. She didn't need him. It just griped her that he'd rejected her.

Anger radiated from her in waves as she stormed away, the scent of her jealousy lingering behind like poison.

Rafe whistled. "Damn, man, you're back in town for a day and you've already ruffled feathers. Plus you've got women chasing you left and right."

"Not women, Ellie." Cabe chuckled sardonically. "But we both know what she wants."

"Jessie Becker had her eyes on you, too," Rafe said with a toothy grin.

"Jessie just wants to protect her family and get me out of town. Period."

Rafe shrugged, then gestured toward Ellie. "I don't know about Jessie, but you're right about Ellie. She's always been strong-willed and obsessed with the activist faction. But lately…"

"Lately what?"

"I don't know. But I'd watch out for her." Rafe made a hissing sound between his teeth. "She seems…dangerous. Out of control."

Cabe watched Ellie disappear into the crowd, shaking hands and speaking to the Natives, his gaze latching on to her long black hair.

He'd collected two long black hairs today at the crime scene. Did they belong to Ellie?

Chapter Four

Could Ellie's obsession have festered out of control?
Could she be a killer?

She was outspoken, opinionated, a voracious advocate for the Native American faction.

Except that she bordered on conniving and controlling, a lethal combination that could entice her to cross the line.

The activists sometimes forgot the bigger picture and became a negative force regarding their own people because their protests only roused anger and unrest instead of building peace and harmony between the two factions. Some even adhered to the old beliefs so strictly that they ignored the benefits of modern society.

It was the twenty-first century. Shouldn't these prejudices have died by now?

"Are you going to see your father while you're here?" Running Horse asked quietly.

Cabe met his gaze. No judgment there. Just an understanding that they were both straddling a fragile fence, especially in light of the recent revelations in Comanche Creek.

"I doubt he wants to see me."

"You might be surprised."

Cabe's wide jaw clamped. "What? Is something wrong with my father?"

Despite his resentment toward his father and the ugly conversation they'd had the last time he'd seen him, he didn't want to hear that his father was ill. He was…the only family Cabe had left.

At one time, he'd wanted nothing more than his respect. To make him proud. He'd thought becoming a Ranger might accomplish that, but the fantasy had died a sudden and fast death when he'd left the reservation.

"Rafe?"

"No," Rafe said. "It's just that you're here. And it might be time to mend broken fences."

Cabe shrugged, resorting as he always did, back to his job. "I have my hands full right now."

Besides, his father might be in cahoots with Ellie and the Natives who were ready to lynch Jonah Becker and Jerry Collier for cheating them out of their land.

A noise behind them snagged his attention, and he spotted Charla Whitley making a beeline toward him, her makeup stark beneath the lights of the room, a half-dozen silver bracelets jangling on her arm.

She offered him a conspiratorial smile but he detected a secret agenda. Part Native American, he'd heard she collected cultural artifacts and sold them on the side. She had also worked with her husband, Billy, as his administrative assistant, and might have been involved in the illegal land deal.

"Watch out for that one, too," Running Horse muttered. "Charla had a breakdown after Billy died and threatened to kill herself. She was admitted to the psych hospital for a while, and was just released."

Cabe gave a clipped nod. He didn't know whom he could trust in this town.

Her ruby red lips curved into a smile. "Cabe Navarro, I'm glad those Rangers finally brought in one of our own. We need someone working for us."

Once again, he felt compelled to reiterate his neutral position. "I'm a Sergeant, a Texas Ranger, Charla. I'm here to uncover the truth, and get justice for all the murder victims, not take sides."

"Of course you are, Cabe." Charla raked her blood-red fingernails across his arm. "I'm relieved you'll be investigating Billy's death. I know he didn't kill himself or commit those murders."

"You and Billy were married a long time, weren't you?" Cabe asked.

"It seems like forever." Tears pooled in her eyes. "And I miss him so badly I can't sleep at night. I…just can't believe he's gone."

"You said you didn't believe he killed himself. Why?"

She twisted her mouth in thought, dabbing at her eyes with a tissue. "Because he wanted to know who killed Marcie as bad as the rest of us. She was smearing his name with those allegations about the land deal."

"But the papers are convincing," Cabe said. "It looks like Billy faked the documents to make it appear that Jonah's ancestors owned the land."

"Billy wouldn't cheat anyone, much less the Comanches," Charla said firmly. "He knew I was faithful to our people."

Cabe made a grunting sound. He wasn't falling for Charla's innocent act. "But I'm sure Jonah paid Billy well for his help. Money can drive people to do things they might not normally do."

Irritation made the lines around her eyes stretch thin. "You sound like you think Billy was guilty, Cabe. Maybe Trace Becker is right. You're playing both sides."

"I already explained my position, Charla. As a matter of fact, I need to ask you about those artifacts in question. The ones you confiscated from Becker's land and sold."

Charla's cheeks turned a ruddy red. "Don't tell me you think I had something to do with all this."

Cabe narrowed his eyes. "Why would you steal from your own people, Charla? Those artifacts should have been left with the dead, or returned to the Comanche Nation."

"I only sold two items and they went to a true collector of Native American artifacts," she said haughtily. "And at the time, I believed I'd made a legitimate deal."

She'd admitted to selling them. Maybe he could push her into confessing more… "So you sold them, then when the truth about their origin came to light, you killed that antiquities broker to keep him quiet. Then you killed Marcie—"

Charla lips twisted into a snarl. "How dare you accuse me of such a thing."

"As far as I'm concerned, everyone in this town is a suspect, Charla. Neither race nor sex is going to factor into the equation when I find the killer. Caucasian or

Comanche, they're going to pay." Cabe pinned her with his eyes. "Now, I'm going to need the name and contact information for the buyer of those artifacts, along with a description of the items."

Charla fidgeted. "I don't have that with me."

"Then get it together. I'll drop by your house tomorrow and pick it up."

She swung around to leave, but he grabbed her arm. "And, Charla, don't you dare warn that buyer I'm coming. If he's gotten rid of the artifacts when I arrive, I'm holding you responsible."

Charla clenched her beaded purse strap with a white-knuckled grip. "Just because you left Comanche Creek, you think you're better than us. But you're not, Cabe. You're worse because you have no loyalty to your family or friends, much less your heritage."

Spinning around on her high-heel boots, she stormed away, her heavy perfume wafting in a cloud behind her.

Cabe almost laughed at her audacity as he watched her meet up with Shane Tolbert at the door. Tolbert placed his hand on her back, and they bowed their heads in conversation as they walked outside.

Just how close were those two? Could they have conspired to carry out the murders?

And why would Shane's father risk jail by setting fire to that cabin on Dead Man's Road, and shoot at a Ranger and Sheriff Hardin if he believed his son was innocent?

NIGHT HAD SET IN, EVENING shadows cloaking the street outside the building as Jessie stepped outside the courthouse. She spotted Trace and Ellie Penateka talking near Ellie's Jeep Wrangler across the street and frowned. Their noses were almost touching. They almost looked…friendly.

Ellie was well-known for her strong opinions around Comanche Creek, and one of the last people she would expect to be friends with Trace. Then again, maybe Ellie thought that if she could convince Trace to side with the Comanches, then he could sway the opposing faction in town.

As if she suddenly sensed Jessie watching, Ellie tilted her head, pivoted and locked gazes with her. A nasty look of disdain curled her mouth, sending a chill up Jessie's spine. Then Trace said something to her, and Ellie jerked away and bolted for her car.

What exactly was going on between them?

Before she could go after Trace to ask him, Mayor Sadler lumbered up on her heels. "Jessie, wait."

She tensed, pasting on a smile when all she wanted to do was drive back to the ranch, take a hot shower and go to bed. But the mayor and her father were friends, and she appreciated his loyalty. Still, she wondered if Mayor Sadler had helped soothe the way for her father to make the land deal. He was popular and had connections in the town that ran deep.

He tugged up his pants, which were riding low below his belly. "How's your daddy doing? I thought he'd be here tonight."

Jessie's chest squeezed with pain. Everyone else was probably expecting him to appear as well, especially since her father's name and future were at stake. It wasn't like Jonah to back down from a fight or not solve a problem himself.

She hated to lie, but there was no other way. "Dad's fine, just tired tonight."

The mayor's brows furrowed. "I hope all this controversy isn't wearing on him."

More than you know, Jessie thought.

Sergeant Cabe Navarro stepped from the building then, his broad shoulders stretching across that white shirt as he stopped to survey the streets. His black Stetson shielded those dark enigmatic eyes, his shoulder-length hair held at the nape of his neck by a leather thong. With that rugged tough exterior, the feral power in his stance and his stark cheekbones, he looked like an ancient Native American warrior, as if he should be carrying a bow and arrow instead of a gun.

For a moment, an odd fluttering started in her belly, a feeling she hadn't experienced before.

Cabe Navarro was strong, masculine, tough as nails…and sexy as all get-out. Heaven help her, but she wanted to forget he was a Ranger, and give in to the attraction she felt stirring in her chest.

But that Silver Star of Texas badge he wore on his chest like a mantra gleamed in the moonlight, reminding her they were on opposite sides.

"No," Jessie said. "Although having those Rangers on the land is unsettling. I was hoping by now they would have arrested Marcie's killer and stop hassling us."

"It's hard to believe we have a killer running around Comanche Creek," the mayor muttered. "I don't like all this trouble in my town. And I don't like that Navarro guy. I think your brother may be right. He may be playing both sides."

"But I was with him today on the ranch when he found another body," Jessie said. "So he may be right about the burial grounds."

The mayor leaned closer and spoke in a conspiratorial whisper. "That may be true, but I'm afraid he's gunning for your daddy. You don't want to see Jonah go to jail, do you?"

Panic stabbed Jessie. "No, of course not."

The mayor's bushy eyebrows rose. "You're a pretty girl, Jessie. Maybe you can convince Navarro that your father is innocent, that Billy pulled the wool over his eyes when he forged those documents."

Jessie chewed her lip, uneasy at his tone. Was he suggesting she cozy up to the Ranger and sleep with him to alleviate suspicion from her father?

Did Mayor Sadler know something more about the deal than he'd let on?

CABE SPOTTED JESSIE talking to the mayor, and wished he could hear their conversation. Were they plotting how to cover for Jonah?

Tomorrow he'd speak to Becker himself. But first, he'd obtain that warrant for a sample of Jonah's blood and DNA. Hopefully the lab would have the results of the red clay on the Double B, and he would know if it matched the blood used in the ritualistic burials. If that blood matched Jonah Becker's, he'd throw the rich old man in jail.

And if Jessie had covered for him…

He'd have to arrest her, too.

That thought made his gut knot, but he pushed the disturbing feeling aside and strode toward Jessie and the mayor. He'd come to Comanche Creek to catch a killer, soothe ruffled feathers and right the land deal, and nothing could deter him from doing that job.

Not the mayor, or Ellie, who'd been staging protest marches in front of the county land office, or the sexy Jessie Becker, who could disarm a man with her sultry eyes.

Still, another problem nagged at him. When the killer was arrested and the town settled down, the spirits of the dead who'd been disturbed needed to be put back to rest.

How the hell could he do that?

Your father would know how.

No…the last thing his father wanted was to see him.

The mayor shot him an angry look, then turned and walked toward the parking lot.

Jessie folded her arms in a defensive gesture as he approached.

"That meeting went well," he said sarcastically.

Her small laugh of agreement rang with understanding. But that laugh made him wonder what she would sound like if she wasn't being sardonic.

"There hasn't been a murder around here in over a decade, so it's normal for people to be on edge."

"True. And it's worse knowing the killer might be their very own neighbor."

"I'm sorry about Trace," Jessie said.

Sympathy mixed with admiration for her. "You're not responsible for your brother's behavior, Jessie."

She relaxed slightly as if to thank him for not judging her based on Trace's rude actions.

His stomach growled, reminding him he hadn't eaten all day, and he gestured toward the diner. "Hungry?"

She shrugged. "Are you inviting me to join you for dinner?"

A small smile tilted the corner of his mouth. "Why not? Concerned that it's bad for your image to be seen with me?"

She made a dismissive sound. "Who the heck cares about image? Half the men in town believe I'm a daddy's girl, the other half think I'm a tomboy."

"Because you can ride and work a ranch?"

A breeze blew a strand of hair across her face, and she brushed in back. The gesture was so damn feminine that it made his groin ache.

"Yeah. That and the fact that I can shoot as well as they can."

"Those guys are blind *and* idiots," Cabe muttered. Hell, she was smart, tough and a marksman. He'd like to see her with a gun.

Or with a rope, maybe tying him down...

Sweat exploded on this brow. What the hell was he thinking?

Annoyed at himself for letting his thoughts stray to dangerous places, he clamped his jaw tight. "Only cowards are intimidated by strong women."

A teasing smile flickered in her eyes. "But you're not, Ranger?"

"No way." In fact, he was intrigued.

If a woman could ride a horse the way he knew she could, she sure as hell could ride a man to oblivion.

He quickly blinked away the images that thought triggered and opened the door to the diner. Dammit. He had to keep this conversation professional.

Voices and laughter from the inside dragged him back to reality, and he scanned the room. Judging from the packed booths and tables, half the town had joined here to eat and rehash the meeting. But he shook his head in disgust as he noticed the division in the room.

It was almost as if a visible line had been drawn down the center with the right side filled with the Caucasian faction, the left filled with the Natives.

Both groups glared at him as if they'd like to tar and feather him.

"Want to rethink eating with me?" he mumbled.

She jutted up her dainty chin. "No. As you recall, I'm part of this task force, too."

"Only because of your land," Cabe said stiffly. "So don't lie to me or keep anything from me, Jessie."

Any lightness between them evaporated like water on hot pavement. "And don't railroad my father for something he didn't do."

A tense silence stretched between them as they claimed bar stools at the counter. One of the waitresses, Sally Rainer, approached with a nervous smile, glancing between them curiously.

A hefty man wearing jeans, battered boots and black leather gloves took the bar seat on the other side of him. Behind him, voices of disgust rumbled, the discontent palpable.

"Hey there, Sergeant Navarro," Sally said. "Glad to have you back in town."

He grunted. "Not everybody feels that way."

She slid two glasses of sweet tea in front of them, then handed them menus. "Some of us know better," she said. "And I, for one, am relieved you're here. We need a neutral party who understands both sides, don't we, Jessie?"

"Yes, we do," Jessie said pointedly.

Cabe flattened his hands on the counter. "Why can't everyone see that it's not about sides? Comanche Creek should be working as one united community, especially right now."

Sally patted his hand. "Honey, you're right. It's about right and wrong. And I have faith you'll see that justice is served, and help piece this town back together. Now what will you two have for supper?"

Cabe ordered the cubed steak and gravy and Jessie surprised him by doing the same. So she didn't eat rabbit food like some women these days.

He swallowed a big swig of tea then wiped his mouth with the back of his hand. "Tell me what you know about Charla Whitley."

Jessie traced a water droplet on her glass with her finger. "Charla is like a chameleon. She changes color and personality to suit the mood."

"You don't trust her?"

"Not as far as I could throw her."

He liked the way she spoke her mind. "Did she and Billy get along?"

Jessie toyed with her napkin. "As far as I know, why?"

He shrugged. "If Billy didn't commit suicide, then someone killed him."

Her mouth opened in surprise. "You think Charla killed Billy?"

"I don't know," Cabe said. "I'm just asking the obvious questions."

Jessie took a sip of tea and seemed to consider his comment as Sally slid the steaming plates of food in front of them. He dug in, still waiting on Jessie's response.

Finally, she set down her tea. "They seemed well suited," she said. "I know she worked for him and denied knowing the artifacts were stolen."

"She could be lying. Maybe she killed that antiquities broker, Phillips, and Marcie. Billy could have found out, and threatened to turn her in."

She scooped up a bite of mashed potatoes. "I guess it's possible."

Voices stirred around them, the man wearing the gloves got up and left, and Cabe followed his gaze as he disappeared outside. He would have to question most of the locals in town, and he wouldn't be making friends. He'd be adding more enemies to his list.

And God knew, he had enough of those that the shooter today could have been someone from Comanche Creek, or someone else he'd crossed in the past.

Another reason he couldn't get involved with a woman or let one distract him. He had to stay on his toes.

Suddenly a disturbance sounded from outside. Loud voices, arguing, other voices cheering them on.

"Fight, fight, fight!" male voices shouted.

Several patrons in the restaurant jumped up and dove outside to watch.

Sally shot him a panicked look, and he threw down some cash, and rushed to the door. Jessie raced outside on his tail. "What's happening?"

"Stay back," he warned.

The moment he stepped onto the sidewalk, he knew the situation was volatile.

A mixture of older teens, Caucasian, Hispanic and Native, were squared off in the street, circling each other like bloodhounds out for fresh meat.

"You people are trying to cheat us just like you did hundreds of years ago!" a dark-skinned Native boy shouted.

"The land belongs to us now," a tall kid with pale skin snarled.

"Fight, fight, fight!" a group of onlookers shouted.

Cabe stalked to the middle of the group and threw up his hands. "Stop it now!"

"Get out of the way!" another boy shouted.

"Let them settle this," someone yelled.

"No." Cabe raised his gun to fire a warning shot in the air to stop the madness when suddenly a gunshot rang out. The bullet whizzed by Cabe, then Jessie screamed, and he turned to see if she'd been hit.

Chapter Five

Another bullet flew by Cabe's head, and he ran toward Jessie and pushed her behind one of storefront posts. "Are you all right?"

Her breathing sounded choppy, but she nodded. "Where are the shots coming from?"

"I don't know." He quickly conducted a visual of the boys who'd been fighting, but didn't spot a weapon in their hands. In fact, they'd scattered in different directions, rushing to take cover, the fight forgotten. Locals rushed into the diner and raced to their cars in terror. He glanced around for the mayor, but he had disappeared.

Jerry Collier, Jonah Becker's lawyer, was ducking around back to the parking lot behind the sheriff's office.

Where was Trace Becker?

Sheriff Hardin stepped from the city hall, assessing the situation, his gun drawn. A quick glance at Cabe, and Cabe shook his head indicating he hadn't spotted the shooter.

Squinting through the glare of the streetlight, Cabe scanned the storefronts, the nearby alley, then checked the rooftops. A movement above the hardware store caught his attention, and he gestured toward Hardin with a crook of his finger.

Hardin gave a slow nod, and Cabe grabbed Jessie's arm. "Stay put and stay down. I'm going after him."

Jessie clutched the column. "Be careful."

He ducked and raced along the storefronts toward the hardware store while Hardin covered him. The shadow moved again, running toward the back of the building, and Cabe fired a shot. Hardin darted across the street, running toward him.

"He's going around the back." Cabe gestured to the right. "Let's split up and maybe we can corner him. I'll take that side."

Hardin waved his gun. "I'll go left."

They quickly split. Cabe saw a couple of teens huddled in the alley, as he circled to the right, and motioned for them to run toward the front of the building. A white pickup truck darted from the parking lot and raced away from town, tires screeching. The sound of a garbage can being knocked over echoed a few feet away, and he spotted someone dashing through the alley in the back.

Hardin met him behind the hardware store. "Someone just ran into the alley," Cabe said.

Hardin gave a clipped nod. "I called Deputy Tolbert to search inside the store. I'll check the roof."

Holding his gun beside him, Cabe jogged down the alley until it opened up to a side street that led to a cluster of dilapidated apartments. Sweat slid down his brow as he searched the dark shadows, the nooks and crannies between the apartment buildings.

Then he spotted the figure, and his pulse pounded. Trace Becker.

Had Trace been shooting at him?

Becker paused and leaned against the staircase railing of one of the units, panting and checking over his shoulder.

Inching toward the first building, Cabe held his gun at the ready, then closed the distance, making certain to keep his footfalls light to avoid detection. A dog appeared from the patio next door, and Cabe put out his hand, speaking softly to soothe the animal so it wouldn't bark or attack.

Becker started to move again, but Cabe vaulted from behind the apartment and pointed his gun at the man's chest.

Trace's eyes went wild with panic, and he threw up his hands in a defensive gesture. "Don't shoot," Trace screeched.

Cabe clenched his jaw. "Spread your legs and keep your hands above your head."

"Look, Ranger—"

"Do it," Cabe ordered.

Becker's brown eyes flicked with a nasty snarl, but he complied. Cabe quickly patted him down, searching for a weapon.

"I didn't do anything. I'm not armed," Becker growled.

Cabe removed handcuffs from his belt, jerked Becker's arms behind him and snapped the cuffs around his wrists.

"Dammit, take it easy, you son—"

"Shut up," Cabe said, practically daring him to mouth

off, "or I will slap a resisting arrest charge on you and throw your butt in a cell."

Trace stiffened. "You can't arrest me. I haven't done anything."

"I can and I will," Cabe said through gritted teeth. The guy needed to spend a night in jail just for being a smart-ass bastard. "What did you do with the gun, Becker?"

Trace grunted as Cabe spun him around and took him by the arm. "I told you I'm not armed," Trace shouted, "and I didn't fire those shots."

"Then why were you running?"

Becker hissed out a breath. "Because I figured you'd try to pin the shooting on me after what happened in the city hall."

Cabe narrowed his eyes, scrutinizing Trace's every movement. Funny how Trace and Jessie were siblings, but were nothing alike. She was strong and tough and attractive, where he just looked smarmy.

And dammit, if Becker hadn't fired at him, then Trace's dash to escape had sidetracked him from chasing after the real shooter.

Cabe shoved Becker in front of him, his gun still trained on the man's back. "Then you won't mind coming me with me and letting me process your hands for gunshot residue."

JESSIE'S HEART POUNDED when she spotted Ranger Navarro shoving her brother in front of him as they emerged from behind the hardware store.

The shooting had ceased, the streets had grown quiet as people dispersed, and Sheriff Hardin appeared from the opposite direction. Deputy Shane Tolbert exited the front of the hardware store, a pinched look on his face.

Dear God. Trace was handcuffed. Was her brother the shooter?

The men met in front of the courthouse, and she rushed to join them, frantic to hear what was going on.

"Did you see anyone?" Ranger Navarro asked the sheriff.

"No." Sheriff Hardin arched a questioning brow at Trace but turned to Deputy Tolbert first.

"Shane, what about inside the building?"

Deputy Tolbert shook his head. "I checked the store, the offices, the storage room and the back staircase. "Nobody was inside but the owner, Henry. When he heard the gunfire, he locked himself in his office."

The sheriff cocked his head toward Trace. "What happened?"

Jessie held her breath. She knew Trace would go to great lengths to protect their father, but would he actually resort to murder?

"I caught him running away in the alley," Ranger Navarro said.

"Was he armed?" Sheriff Hardin asked.

The Ranger shook his head. "No. But he could have stashed the gun someplace. Maybe the alley, a garbage can. Somewhere inside the hardware store."

Hardin nodded. "If he did, we'll find it."

"Good," Cabe mumbled. "I'm going to take him and process his hands for GSR."

"You're wasting your time." Trace glared at the Ranger, then at Jessie. "I didn't do anything."

"Why were you running then?" Sheriff Hardin asked.

A belligerent look darkened Trace's beady eyes as he flicked his hand toward Cabe. "Because I knew *he* would try to pin the blame on me."

"Stop whining," Ranger Navarro said coldly. "You asked for it. And if you weren't the shooter, then your running caused me to chase you and miss the real perp. I should lock you up for interfering with an investigation."

"That's preposterous," Trace growled.

Jessie crossed her arms. "Where are you taking him?"

"To the jail to process his hands."

"Call Jerry Collier and tell him to meet me at the sheriff's office," Trace said to Jessie. "This guy is not going to railroad me into a cell for something I didn't do."

"Yes, Jessie, call Collier," Cabe said. "I want to question him, too." He turned to the sheriff. "Hardin, escort Becker to a holding cell while I retrieve my crime scene kit from the SUV. I want to search for those bullets before the scene gets any more contaminated than it already has been."

Hardin nodded. "I've decided to ask the mayor to issue a curfew for the residents until this whole mess is cleared up. A shooting in a public place, those boys nearly fighting—this situation is way out of hand."

"Good idea," the Ranger agreed. "We don't want any more casualties just because tempers are running high."

"Meanwhile Deputy Tolbert can start searching for a weapon," Sheriff Hardin said.

The fact that the deputy had been a suspect himself must have troubled Cabe because he cleared his throat and addressed Tolbert. "Do you mind if I see your hands and weapon?"

Tolbert cursed, but extended his hands and flexed his fingers. The Ranger leaned over and examined them, then asked to see his gun. Tolbert removed his Smith and Wesson, checked the safety, then handed it to the Ranger.

Jessie dug in her purse for her cell phone to call Jerry Collier while Navarro examined Tolbert's weapon.

Tolbert glared at Cabe. "See, it hasn't been fired recently."

Cabe checked the magazine clip, then, reloaded it, and handed the weapon back to the deputy.

Tolbert gave a smug grin as he stowed it back in his holster.

"All right," the Ranger said. "Go back to the hardware store and search for a weapon. Check everywhere, including the vents, and the Dumpster outside."

Tolbert scowled as if he disliked taking orders, but must have decided not to push the Ranger's buttons by arguing. Jessie watched the power struggle between the men with trepidation.

Shane Tolbert had always struck her as a hothead. He liked women. Had a quick temper. And he had been infatuated with Marcie. Jessie still wondered about his innocence.

Trace grunted as the sheriff hauled him next door to his office. Even she had to admit that Trace looked suspicious.

She had to protect her family. Not that Trace didn't deserve to be taken down a notch, but it would kill her father if Trace went to jail for murder.

CABE HALFWAY HOPED Trace did turn out to be the shooter, and he could lock the little SOB up. But the look of distress on Jessie's face gnawed at him.

She and Trace might not get along, but arresting Trace—or her father—would definitely upset her world.

Too bad, he thought.

A sliver of guilt wormed its way inside him. Jessie was…innocent.

Either that or she was a damn good actress.

Focus, Cabe. Lives depend on you keeping a clear head. You don't want the body count rising on your watch.

He kept his senses honed for trouble as he rushed to his SUV for his crime kit. The parking lot was near empty now, the town quiet as the shooting had driven most citizens home.

A storm cloud rumbled, making him hurry his footsteps, and he grabbed the kit from his SUV and rushed back to the front of the diner. He pulled on gloves, retrieved a flashlight from the kit and began to scour the street, the sidewalk, the front wall of the diner and storefronts for the bullets and casings. But after half an hour, he came up with nothing.

He closed his eyes, mentally reliving the moment when he'd stepped outside to stop the fight. Jessie had been right behind him, the boys arguing. He'd stepped into the middle of the circle of the boys, then the shot had rung out.

He turned in a wide arc, analyzing their positions, where he'd been standing, how close the bullet had come to his head, then studied the top of the hardware store building. Judging from the angle of the shooter, the distance the bullet had traveled, the line of fire…

His stomach knotted.

Had the shooter been firing at him or Jessie?

The realization that he might not have been the target presented momentary relief as well as surprise, but the fact that Jessie might have been the perp's target disturbed him even more.

Why would someone want to kill Jessie Becker?

Because she had secrets? Because she was protecting her father?

And who wanted her dead?

Trace?

He hissed a breath between clenched teeth, then pivoted, this time focusing on where Jessie had stood, and strode over to the diner's front wall again. He was about six-four, Jessie probably five-five, so this time he skimmed his hand down the wall again, considered the angle of the shot and distance, and shone the flashlight on the surface. About an inch above where Jessie's head would have been, he spotted a break in the plaster.

Muttering a curse, he removed his pocketknife from his jeans pocket, flipped it open and dug the bullet from the wall. Using tweezers, he examined the bullet.

It was warped, but the lab could do wonders these days. He retrieved a bag from his kit, dropped the bullet inside, sealed it and placed it in the kit. Sweat trickled down his neck as he waved the flashlight across the wall again, looking for the second bullet. Nothing.

Rethinking the scene, he remembered he and Jessie

had ducked behind the column for cover. The shooter had obviously tracked their movements. He knelt, spied the broken plaster in the crevice of the wall behind a fake rosebush in front of the diner, and dug it out as well.

After securing it in his crime kit, he headed to the sheriff's office and jail. Jessie Becker sat in a straight chair tapping her foot while she waited.

He gave her a perfunctory look, the camaraderie they'd shared during their meal together lost as business took center stage.

Sheriff Hardin emerged from the back. "Did you find the bullets?"

"Yeah." He removed them from the kit, and signed transfer papers for the courier for chain of evidence to be sent to the lab in Austin.

The sight of Jessie sitting all alone stirred some primal protective instinct inside him that he had to ignore. She had removed her hat and was running her fingers through those red tresses. The movement made his fingers itch to feel the silky strands.

But he couldn't touch her now.

If Trace had shot at them, or at *her*, then he had to be stopped.

He adjusted his hat as he walked past her, then down the short hall connecting the jail cells. He'd let Trace stew a while and talk to Ben Tolbert first.

Cabe found the tired-looking man in the first cell, pacing. "Ben Tolbert?"

Tolbert stopped pacing and glared up at him. "Who are you?"

"Ranger Sergeant Cabe Navarro."

"Another damn outsider," Ben grunted. "I've already given my confession. What do you want?"

"To know why you shot at a Ranger and a cop if your son was innocent."

Tolbert rubbed his bloodshot eyes. "My boy *is* innocent," he said firmly. "But I've been around long enough to know that the law don't always work."

"So you risked your own future by trying to kill a cop?"

"I'm Shane's father. I'd do anything for my boy."

Cabe studied him intently. The man seemed sincere, at least sincere in that he believed in his son's innocence.

Animosity flattened Tolbert's eyes. "Now, unless you came to release me, leave me the hell alone."

Cabe silently cursed. He recognized a dead lead, and Tolbert was one.

Leaving the old man, he walked back to the interrogation room. Trace sat at the table with his arms folded, hatred spewing from his eyes.

"Where's my lawyer?" Trace grumbled.

"You don't need one if you're innocent," Cabe said sharply.

"That's a load of crap," Trace muttered. "I don't trust you or the law in this town. For all I know you volunteered to come here so you could throw your badge around and make life hell for those of us who weren't your buddies when you lived in Comanche Creek before."

Cabe slanted him a steely look. "If you think I give a damn about high school and you idiots, you're a bigger fool than I thought." He gestured at the table. "Now let me see your hands."

The door screeched open, and the sheriff escorted Jerry Collier inside. Collier was a weasel of a guy with dusty gray eyes and sandy hair. His pinched face made him look untrustworthy like the sack of garbage Cabe had expected him to be.

Collier planted his briefcase on the table beside Becker. "What's going on here?"

"I'm Ranger Sergeant Cabe Navarro. Gunshots were fired tonight near the diner. Your client was running from the scene."

Collier's eyes flickered toward Trace, then back to Cabe. "Did he have a weapon on him?"

"No, but we're searching the hardware store, streets and alley now."

"Is he under arrest?"

Cabe swallowed back irritation. "Not officially. He's here for questioning."

Collier nodded. "All right, let's get this over with so he can go home."

"First, I need to process his hands."

Trace twisted his mouth into a grimace, but complied. Cabe studied Becker's palms and fingers, but didn't spot GSR on his skin. Still, he removed a swab from the kit, dabbed it in the chemicals the lab had issued, and brushed it across Trace's hands and fingers. Then he took a DNA swab from Becker's mouth, and bagged and labeled both of them.

Cabe leveled his most intimidating stare at Trace. "Now, tell me again, why you were running down that alley."

Trace shoved his hands down into his lap. "Because I heard the shots, saw you coming and figured you'd blame me."

"Why were you behind the hardware store anyway?" Cabe asked.

"When I heard the commotion in the street, I decided to take a shortcut to my car."

"Sounds logical to me," Collier said. "Now, unless you have enough evidence to arrest him, which you don't, Sergeant, we're done here."

Trace stood, and Collier reached for his briefcase.

Cabe slid a hand to his weapon. "Don't leave town, Becker. And if I find that gun and it has your DNA on it, I will come after you. And this time, no lawyer is going to get you off."

"I should file harassment charges against you," Trace snapped.

Collier herded Trace toward the door. "Let's go, Trace."

Cabe stepped in front of the door and folded his arms. "Just a second, Collier. Where were you when the shooting took place?"

Collier's eyes bulged with outrage. "After your little impromptu meeting, I hid out in my office to escape the mob of activists. I was afraid there might be a riot."

Shooting Cabe a defiant look, Collier shouldered his way past Cabe, and he and Trace rushed down the hall to the front office.

Cabe followed, and saw Jessie jump up to speak to Trace. "I'm going home," Trace said to her. "And if you know what's good for you, Jessie, you'll leave that Comanche alone."

Collier shoved Trace outside, and Jessie glanced up at him just as he walked back into the room.

The wary look she gave him knotted his insides, and he strode toward her and stroked her arm. A tingle shot through him, the need to pull her against him and ease her burdens nearly overwhelming him.

"Be careful, Jessie," he warned in a gruff voice.

A mixture of emotions flickered in her eyes. "I appreciate your concern, Ranger, but I can take care of myself," she said softly.

Her gaze met his, something passing between them, an attraction that completely caught him off guard.

What the hell was wrong with him? He never got tied in knots over a woman.

An almost panicked expression lit her eyes as if she'd read his mind. "I have to go." Then she eased her arm from his hand, and darted out the door.

Anxiety filled him as he spotted Trace standing outside watching through the window. "She can't save you or your daddy if you're guilty," Cabe muttered. "And she can't save your daddy if his blood matches the victims' either."

He just hoped to hell that Jessie wasn't covering for them.

He didn't want to have to arrest her.

TRACE STORMED TOWARD Jessie as soon as she exited the sheriff's office.

"If you aren't going to stay away from the Ranger, at least you could try to sway suspicion from me and Daddy."

Jessie glared at him, tired of his bully ways. "You

need to behave, Trace. If you hadn't practically attacked Cabe at the meeting, he might not be suspicious of you. If he arrests you, it'll be your own damn fault."

"So now you're taking up for him?" Trace said in a nasty tone.

Instead of acknowledging his comment, she rolled her eyes in disgust, then turned and stalked down the sidewalk toward the parking lot and her Jeep. She wouldn't have blamed the Ranger if he'd thrown Trace's butt in jail for the night. Her brother's hotheaded ways would land him in real trouble someday.

If it hadn't already…

A light breeze stirred the trees as she drove back to the ranch, but the Santa Gertrudis roaming the land and horses galloping in the pastures were a comforting sight. Concern for her father overrode her exhaustion, and she stopped by the main house to check on him. But when she entered the house, it was dark.

A note on the kitchen counter from Lolita explained that her father was already in bed. Maybe it was better they talk in the morning anyway. She didn't want to upset him by having to relay that Trace had nearly been arrested.

She gathered the other messages and flipped through them. One of her grooms had reported that a second creek bed in the north end of the ranch was dried up. Odd. What had caused that? A second message asked her to check on one of the quarter horses. The vet had already treated his injured foot, but Jessie had requested that she be informed any time there was a problem.

Wanting to check on him herself, she walked back out to her Jeep and drove over the graveled road to the stables where they housed the quarter horses. She left her hat in the car, jammed her phone in the pocket of her jeans and hiked over to the barn.

The smell of hay and horses soothed her frayed nerves as she entered, the horses whinnying and kicking the walls in greeting. Brown Sugar jammed his nose through the grate of the stall, wanting her attention, and she paused to pet him. "Hey there, sugar. I missed you, too."

She moved down the row of stalls, petting Honey and Pepper as well, then stopped at the last stall to check on Buttercup. She was lying on her side, but lifted her head and looked alert. Jessie unlatched the stall door and slipped inside, then stooped and stroked her back. "How are you feeling, Buttercup? Is that foot getting better?"

Buttercup nudged her head, and Jessie lifted the bandage edge and checked the wound. Already the redness was dissipating, the swelling going down. Relieved, she started to stand but the floor creaked behind her, and the lights went out.

Panic slammed into her, and she scanned the darkness, but suddenly the floor creaked again and a hulking figure lunged toward her. She threw up her hands to ward off the blow, but his hand came down and something sharp and hard slammed into her head.

Pain knifed through her skull, the barn spun in a dizzying circle, then she collapsed into the darkness.

Chapter Six

Cabe was still stewing over Trace's threatening tone with Jessie when the sheriff's cell phone trilled.

Reed snapped it open. "Sheriff Hardin." Pause. "Jesus. All right. I'll send Sergeant Navarro out there now."

Cabe frowned. "What's wrong?"

"That was one of the ranch hands at the Becker place. He found Jessie unconscious in the barn."

Cabe's pulse spiked. Dammit, maybe he'd been right about the shooter targeting her tonight. Had he followed her home, then attacked her?

Or had Trace come after her?

"The ranch hand called an ambulance," Reed said. "You want to check it out while I help Deputy Tolbert search for the gun used in the shooting tonight?"

Cabe was already heading toward the door. "I'm on my way." Perspiration beaded on his neck as he jogged to his Land Rover, jumped in and sped from town. Traffic had definitely died down since the earlier shooting. The quiet of the countryside should have been soothing, but knowing Jessie was hurt fueled his anger.

Why would someone want to kill her? Because of her father's enemies?

Or had she and Trace fought over him?

If that was the case, he'd kill the SOB.

The rumblings in the diner when the two of them had walked in echoed in his head. What if someone in town was riled because they thought she was siding with him?

Miles of scrub brush, mesquites and oaks dotted the landscape as he ate the distance between the town and ranch. The ranch hand who'd found Jessie must have already opened the gate for the ambulance, so he zoomed up to the drive, then veered off onto the dirt road leading to the horse barns.

His headlights flickered up ahead, and he spotted Jessie's Jeep and an old pick-up truck to the side. He raced to a halt, jumped out and hurried into the barn. The smell of hay and horse assaulted him, the sound of the horses' whinnying filling the air.

A craggy-looking man wearing jeans and weathered boots limped toward him, favoring his right foot. "I'm Wilbur. You the law?"

"Ranger Sergeant Navarro. How badly is she hurt?"

"Looks like she took a blow to the head. She's startin' to stir, but I didn't want to move her till the paramedics said it was okay." The old man gestured toward the back stall just as the sound of a siren rent the air. "I'll meet the medics and send them in."

Cabe gave a clipped nod, then strode toward the back stall. His heart pounded as he pushed open the stall door, and saw Jessie lying on her side in the bed of straw. The horse lay beside her, nudging her face with his nose.

Her brilliant red hair was tangled around her, and her face was pale and chalky. He spotted a few droplets of blood in her hair, and knelt to examine her. Gently, he lifted strands of hair away from the wound to judge the depth and severity.

A gash about an inch long marred her scalp, but thankfully the cut didn't look too deep.

"Jessie," he said softly, "can you hear me?"

A low moan sounded, and he gritted his teeth. "It's all right, Jessie," he whispered. "The medics are here now."

Voices rumbled from outside, then closer as the medics hurried into the barn. Cabe stood and moved outside the stall, allowing them access.

One medic checked her pulse while the second one examined her wound. He glanced up with a frown. "Looks like she needs a couple of stitches."

"Her vitals are stable." The second medic glanced up at Cabe. "We'll get the stretcher and transport her to the hospital for X-rays. It's possible she has a concussion."

Cabe nodded. "I'll meet you there. I want to search the barn for the weapon her attacker used."

Maybe he'd get lucky this time and find some other forensics as well.

But his anger mounted as he studied Jessie's pale face and closed eyes, and protective instincts surged to the surface.

From now on, he'd make sure she was safe. No one would ever hurt her again.

JESSIE BLURRED IN AND OUT of consciousness, her head aching as if a jackhammer was pounding her skull. Perspiration trickled down her neck and into her shirt, and she pawed her way through the darkness, struggling to grasp on to something to help her up.

But her body felt weighted and heavy, the air humid, the rumble of a car engine whining in her head.

Where was she? What was going on?

She blinked against the dizziness, pinpoints of light pricking her eyes.

"Just relax, Miss Becker," a strange male voice murmured. "You have a head injury, and you're in an ambulance. We'll be at the hospital soon."

Head injury? Hospital? What happened?

As the ambulance raced along, slowly the events of the night returned. The trip into town. The shooting. The Ranger questioning her brother. Her confrontation with Trace. The attack in the horse stall.

Someone had struck her over the head. But why? Who would want to hurt her?

Trace?

Good God, surely not.

Thoughts of her troubled family taunted her. Did her father know she'd been assaulted?

She prayed he didn't. Bad news would only agitate his condition.

And Trace…he had no reason to be jealous of her.

Her father didn't love her, at least not the way Trace thought. If he had, he never would have allowed her mother to take her away when she was a little girl. He would have insisted on visitation, holidays, but he hadn't, not once.

And her mother—at first, she'd lived in a fantasy

world, believing that her mother had wanted custody because she couldn't live without her. But then she'd jumped from man to man, from city to city, and Jessie had realized that the only reason she'd taken her was to hurt Jonah, and to get the money he regularly sent.

A soul-deep ache rolled through her. No matter what she'd done to impress her parents, she'd never been close to either one of them. Moving back to the ranch had been her attempt to win her father's love.

But then his mind had started slipping away.

And she'd felt more alone than ever.

Ranger Cabe Navarro's strong, chiseled face flashed into her mind. She'd heard his voice in the barn, soothing, husky, sultry, like a hot summer's night washing over her. She closed her eyes and, for just a moment, allowed herself to think that he really cared about her, that he was sliding those muscular arms around her and pulling her to his broad chest.

That his mission might not destroy her family.

That she was lying in his arms, safe and loved, and that someone hadn't just tried to kill her.

THE ODDEST FEELING pressed against Cabe's chest as the ambulance drove away with Jessie. Something akin to fear that he might lose her.

Which was ridiculous. Jessie didn't belong to him, and she never would.

But the night his brother died rose to haunt him, and he couldn't shake the worry that he needed to be by her side.

"Reckon I'll go tell the family about Miss Jessie," Wilbur said.

Cabe nodded. "Did you see anybody when you first got out here?"

Wilbur scratched his chin. "Naw. Weren't no cars here, and it was pitch-dark."

"Did you hear anything? Maybe a car nearby or a horse galloping away?"

Wilbur angled his head in thought. "Not that I recall. Don't know how long Miss Jessie had been out, but I saw her Jeep and went inside. It was quiet, that kind of spooky quiet where you know something is wrong." He worked his mouth side to side as if he had a wad of tobacco in his cheek. "You know what I mean?"

He knew exactly what he meant. Instincts. "Yes, sir. Then what happened?"

"Then I checked to see if she was breathing. Thank God she was." He raked a hand over his scraggly hair. "So I called for an ambulance."

"How long have you worked for the Beckers?" Cabe asked.

"Half my life. Mr. Jonah's been good to me. He's not as tough as everyone thinks." The old man shifted and rubbed at his leg as if it was aching. "So if you think I'd hurt Miss Jessie, you're wrong. I love that little girl like she was my own. Her coming home was the best thing ever happened to her daddy."

Sincerity rang in the old man's voice, the affection he felt for the family obvious. "All right, Wilbur. Let me know if you think of anything else."

"Sure thing. Now you find the creep that hurt Miss Jessie. That little lady don't deserve this."

No, she didn't.

Wilbur flicked his hand in a wave, then limped toward his truck.

Dragging his mind back to the task at hand, Cabe retrieved his flashlight and kit from his SUV, then paused to pat the palomino in the stall.

The animal rolled its head sideways, pawing with his uninjured foot as if to say he was upset about Jessie as well. "Don't worry. I'll find out who hurt her, fella."

Cabe pulled on latex gloves, then swept his flashlight across the barn, digging through the straw and wood shavings scattered on the floor. He spent the next half an hour searching the barn, the garbage, the storage room. He methodically examined the grooming tools, searching for blood on the brushes and hoof picks, then searched the neighboring box stalls.

Finally he discovered a hammer that had been dropped down into the stall next to the one where Jessie had been attacked. Blood dotted the hammerhead, so he bagged it to send to the lab. Another sweep-through of the stall, and he spotted a bracelet wedged between the cracks of the wooden slats.

A Native American gold bracelet with garnets embedded in a pattern symbolizing the Morning Star.

The Morning Star was the brightest on the horizon at dawn. Natives revered it as a spirit and most Pueblos honored it as a kachina. The star also symbolized courage and purity of spirit. According to the Ghost Dance Religion, it represented the coming renewal of tradition and resurrection of heroes of the past.

Unease tightened Cabe's chest. He'd seen this bracelet before.

It belonged to Ellie Penateka.

Good God. Had Ellie attacked Jessie?

JESSIE ROUSED IN AND OUT of consciousness as the doctor examined her head. "Miss Becker, you're going to need a couple of stitches. Then we're going to do X-rays and a CAT scan."

She nodded miserably. All she wanted to do was go home.

Or talk to Ranger Navarro and see if he'd found out who had assaulted her.

Her head was throbbing, so she closed her eyes while the doctor cleaned the wound and stitched her. The ride down the elevator for the X-ray and CAT scan was bumpy and made her nauseated. A claustrophobic feeling engulfed her in the cylinder, and she clenched her hands by her sides, willing herself to remain calm. She was strong and tough. She would not fall apart in the hospital.

Finally the lab technicians rolled her from the machine. Perspiration coated her skin, and she gasped for fresh air.

"We'll take you to a room now to rest," the tech assured her.

Jessie clenched the handrail. "I want to go home."

He gave her a sympathetic smile. "The doctor will have to read your tests first."

Frustrated, she massaged her temple while they helped her into a wheelchair and an orderly rolled her back to the elevator. The scents of antiseptic and alcohol flowed through the halls, the droning sound of machinery grating on her nerves.

The orderly dropped her at the nurses' station on the

second floor, and a plump nurse with white hair pushed her toward a room. "Come on, honey, let's settle you in bed so you can rest."

"I hate hospitals." Jessie tried to stand, but a dizzy spell sent the room swirling, and she had to reach out for help to steady herself.

The nurse caught her arm and helped her to the bed. "Take it easy."

Jessie slid beneath the covers, still struggling for control. She was accustomed to taking care of everyone else, not being vulnerable and needy. "I've been stitched up, X-rayed and had a CAT scan, so why can't I go home now?"

"Honey, nobody likes hospitals," the nurse murmured as she adjusted the pillows. "But the doctor insists that you stay under observation for the night."

"But I would rest better at home," Jessie argued.

"Listen, Miss Becker." The nurse's voice grew firm. "It's already midnight. Just go to sleep, and in the morning you can go home."

Jessie clutched the sheets to her, feeling guilty for being a problem, but still anxious. The last thing she wanted was for her father to find out that she'd been attacked on the ranch.

He was in bed when she'd stopped by earlier. Surely Ranger Navarro wouldn't disturb him in the middle of the night...

CABE DIDN'T CARE IF IT WAS the middle of the night. He was going to talk to Ellie and find out what the hell was going on.

The land grew more barren as he left the town and drove to Ellie's pueblo-style house bordering on the edge of the reservation. Apache oaks flanked her property, and bluebonnets swayed from her flower bed. Ellie's place had always boasted of their culture, but her obsession with her cause had colored her tolerance of others who weren't so strong-minded.

Essentially, she liked to stir trouble for trouble's sake. And she had a political agenda.

He had zero tolerance for that kind of behavior— the reason he'd walked away from her and never looked back.

Her small gold sedan was parked in the drive, and a faint light glowed from the bedroom. He rolled his shoulders as he climbed from his SUV and walked up the limestone path to her house. If she hadn't attacked Jessie tonight and was sleeping, she was going to be pissed that he'd disturbed her. And even more so that he considered her a suspect.

But her anger was something he'd live with.

He raised his fist and knocked twice, a light breeze rustling the trees as he waited. A minute later, he knocked again, then saw the kitchen light flicker on, and heard shuffling inside.

"It's Cabe, Ellie, open up."

The peephole opened, and Ellie's eyes widened as she recognized him. "Cabe, what are you doing here?"

"We need to talk," Cabe said.

The click of the lock turning sounded in the quiet of the night, then the door swung open. Ellie tucked a strand of her hair behind her ear, then tied the belt to her satin robe. Her eyes looked blurry, as though she might have been sleeping.

"Cabe, it's late. What's going on?"

"Where were you tonight?"

An instant spark of anger darkened her brown eyes. "You saw me at the meeting, Cabe."

"What did you do after you left?"

She pursed her lips. "I met with some of the supporters of our faction at the barbecue place down the street, then came home."

"What time was that?"

She shrugged and glanced at the clock on her wall. "About nine, I guess. Why are you asking all these questions?"

"You heard the shooting in town. Do you own a gun, Ellie?"

She stiffened. "No. And I was with my friends when that fight broke out. We stayed inside until it was over."

That fact could easily be checked out. "Let me see your hands."

Her eyebrow rose. "What?"

"Just let me see your hands."

She gave him a withering look. "You've got to be kidding, Cabe. I knew you'd crossed the line, but now you're actually turning against us. Against me." She shook her head. "And here I thought we were friends."

"I'm not turning against anyone," Cabe spoke through gritted teeth. "I'm just doing my job."

He lifted her hands and examined them for GSR, but detected no visible signs.

"Satisfied?" she asked bitterly.

"Not yet," he said, ignoring her condemning glare. "You didn't happen to drive out to the Becker ranch, did you?"

"Cabe, why are you asking me these questions?" she asked in a testy voice. "What happened?"

"Jessie Becker was attacked tonight in the barn."

Ellie gasped. "And you think I attacked her?" Hurt crossed her face. "Why in the world would I attack Jessie Becker?"

He steeled himself against her. "Because of her father."

Ellie waved a dismissive hand. "That's ridiculous. I may be an activist but you know I'm not violent." Her lips thinned into a pouty frown. "I can't believe you'd even suggest such a thing, not after the past we shared."

A past that he couldn't allow to interfere with the case.

Pinning her with a stony expression that had intimidated men twice his size, he removed the bagged bracelet he'd found in the barn stall and held it up. "Then why did I find your bracelet in the stall where Jessie was attacked?"

Chapter Seven

Cabe watched Ellie fidget. "It is your bracelet, isn't it, Ellie?"

She chewed her bottom lip, but her gaze lifted to him, a pleading look in her eyes. "You know it is, Cabe. My grandmother gave it to me."

He nodded. "Then why was it in the stall where Jessie was attacked?"

Ellie's face paled slightly, then she gulped and seemed to recover. "There is a logical explanation."

He arched a brow, waiting, his jaw tight. "I'm listening."

"I said I could explain. But I'd rather not." She pressed a hand to the side of her cheek. "It's... personal."

Impatience made him hiss. "Listen, Ellie, I don't give a damn how personal it is. I'm investigating an assault and attempted murder. So if you have a good explanation, you'd better cough it up."

Ellie clamped her teeth over her lip and glanced around nervously. "I *was* out at the Becker place, but not tonight."

"Then when?"

She shrugged. "A couple of evenings ago."

Cabe crossed his arms, suspicious. "What were you doing there?"

Again she glanced over her shoulder, and it struck him that she might not be alone. Was someone in her bedroom?

"Ellie?"

"I went to see Trace."

"Trace? Why? Did you think you could convince him to incriminate his father and turn over the land?"

A slight hesitation. "Not exactly."

"Stop stalling, Ellie, and spit it out."

A long-suffering sigh escaped her. "I've been having an affair with Trace."

Shock bolted through him, ending in a chuckle of disbelief. "Try again."

She raked her gaze over him, angry, defiant, challenging. "Don't act so surprised, Cabe. Do you really think I've been sitting around pining for you?"

"No," he said dryly. "I thought you and Daniel Taabe had a thing."

She shrugged. "Sometimes opposites attract."

"Right. Or maybe you have another agenda. Maybe you're trying to seduce him into helping your cause." That sounded more likely.

"I resent your implication," Ellie said.

"And so do I." The male voice came from behind her, at the door to Ellie's bedroom.

Cabe muttered a curse as Trace Becker sauntered toward Ellie. "You've been listening?" Cabe said.

Becker swung an arm around Ellie. "Damn right I

have. And Ellie was with me tonight, so there's no way she attacked Jessie."

Cabe narrowed his eyes. The two of them were providing each other with alibis—he didn't like it. "Some brother you are. You aren't even going to ask if your sister is all right?"

Trace's bony shoulders lifted. "I figure she is or you would have said she was dead."

Cabe fisted his hands by his side. Trace's tone suggested it wouldn't have bothered him if his sister had died.

"I also found two long black hairs out at the site where that Native body was buried. They look like yours, Ellie."

Ellie huffed. "I was not at the burial site."

"Then let me take a sample of your hair for comparison, to eliminate you as a suspect of course."

Ellie muttered a sound of disbelief, then reached up and yanked out a strand of hair. "Go to hell, Cabe."

She dropped the black strand into his palm, then slammed the door in his face.

Cabe carried the hair to his SUV, bagged and labeled it to send to the lab. The lights flicked off inside, and he imagined Trace and Ellie sliding back in bed together.

Not that he cared who Ellie slept with.

But the fact that they'd hooked up raised questions in his mind.

Was Trace the one playing both sides, maybe to get back at his father for something?

Would Ellie and Trace lie to protect each other? And if they had been in cahoots, what exactly was their agenda?

JESSIE DRIFTED IN AND OUT of a fitful sleep, but the sound of the door squeaking open made her jerk awake, and she blinked trying to distinguish the shadow in the doorway.

Had the person who'd attacked her come here to hurt her again?

Fear clogged her throat, and she threw the covers off her, ready to run.

"It's okay, Jessie. It's me."

The voice—deep, throaty, unerringly male, as potently enticing as his big body. And his scent…like musk and man and sex.

She remembered him soothing her as the ambulance had arrived and had clung to that voice.

"Jessie?" He moved toward her, with silent steps that emanated an air of power and strength.

She exhaled shakily and reached for the covers with a trembling hand, once again feeling naked and exposed.

And more vulnerable than she had in her entire life.

Because she was attracted to this dark-skinned Ranger. More attracted than she'd been to a man in years.

That thought terrified her the most.

She could not fall prey to every sexy man's charms like her mother. And she especially couldn't hop into bed with a man who was determined to destroy her father and the last chance she had of becoming a part of his life.

But as Cabe grew nearer, and she inhaled his scent again, her chest clenched with the need to whisper his name and beg him to stay with her. To confess that she didn't want to be alone.

Not in the dark in this hospital bed knowing that someone had tried to kill her.

He stopped beside her bed, towering over and looking down at her with those brooding, deep brown eyes. Eyes that had seen more than his share of pain and sorrow.

Eyes that had detected spirits on the land in question.

Eyes that could steal her soul—and her heart if she wasn't careful.

"I didn't mean to frighten you," he said gruffly. "How are you feeling?"

Sweet, tender, erotic sensations momentarily numbed the pain in her head at the sound of his concerned tone. She had to clear her throat to speak.

"I'm all right."

He traced a gentle finger into her hair toward the wound. "Headache?"

"A little," she said quietly.

For a moment, it felt as if the two of them were cocooned into the room, as if nothing could touch them or come between them. As if the world and all its problems had faded away.

She wanted the moment to last. To be real.

For the world to disappear. For the murders to be solved. And for Cabe Navarro to stand before her just as a man. Not a Ranger in charge of the case in a town where their two worlds divided them.

"I'm sorry, Jessie." Sincerity laced his voice. "You don't deserve to be in the middle of this mess."

For some reason she didn't understand, tears burned her eyes. Embarrassed, she tried to blink them away, but he must have noticed because he dragged the corner chair over beside the bed, then sat down.

"This is ridiculous," she said, hating her weakness. "I'm not usually so emotional."

"It's natural," Cabe murmured. "You were attacked tonight."

She twisted her hands in the sheets. "You didn't talk to my father, did you?"

"No. Wilbur was going to stop by your house."

"Oh, gosh. I don't want to upset my father."

"Ahh, Jessie." He brushed a strand of hair from her forehead. "Always protecting others, aren't you?"

"That's what families do," she said softly.

"Not always." His expression grew hard. "Do you want me to go?"

A pang of panic went through her chest. "No. I...don't like hospitals. When I was little I got pneumonia, and my mother left me alone for days."

His angular jaw tightened. "She didn't stay with you or visit?"

"No. Her social life was more important." She shook her head, battling bitterness at the memory. God, why was she being such a baby? She'd never told anyone how much that experience had hurt.

He dropped his gaze to her hands, where she'd knotted them in the sheets, then pulled one hand into his big palm. "I'll stay right here and hold your hand all night if you want."

A tingle of awareness ripped through her. "You don't have to do that, Cabe."

Suddenly he stood, walked to the window and looked

out as if he needed to put distance between them. Immediately she missed his closeness. His touch. The connection she'd felt.

"I'm in charge of this case. The person who attacked you might return any time."

A shiver rippled through her, disappointment on its heels. So he wasn't staying out of concern, but because of his job.

She had to remember that.

"Did you get a look at your assailant?" he asked.

"No, the lights went out and he hit me from behind."

He scrubbed a hand through his hair. "Your ranch hand claimed he didn't see anyone either. Do you trust him?"

"Wilbur?" Jessie gave a soft laugh. "With my life. He's like a second father to me." Or maybe a real one.

"I found a hammer that appears to have been the weapon the attacker used. It had blood on it, so I dropped it at the sheriff's office to be couriered to the lab for analysis. Maybe this perp messed up and left a print."

Jessie considered that. "Maybe."

His tone grew darker. "There's something else."

Cold dread filled her. Did he think Trace had attacked her? "What?"

"I found a bracelet in the stall that belonged to Ellie Penateka."

"Ellie? I don't understand. When was she at the barn?"

A sliver of moonlight playing through the window glinted off his strong jaw. "I went to her house and asked her that myself. She claims she and your brother are having an affair."

Shock momentarily robbed Jessie's breath. "Ellie and Trace? You've got to be kidding."

"I didn't believe it either," Cabe said. "But Trace was there. He came out of Ellie's bedroom, and they gave each other alibis for tonight."

Jessie frowned. "I saw them talking after the meeting, but it looked as if they were arguing."

He chuckled sarcastically. "They obviously made up."

Jessie contemplated the implications of Ellie and Trace being together. Trace had been furious when Jessie had showed up at the ranch and announced she was moving back in. He and her father had also argued about the land deal. But Trace had arranged it.

And Trace was worried about losing the ranch to *her.*

Would he team up with Ellie to sabotage her father? No, that didn't make sense…

Unless Trace wanted to hurt their father. Unless he thought that if Jonah went to jail, he would inherit the ranch…

CABE'S GUT PINCHED at the worry on Jessie's face. Maybe he should have waited until she'd recovered before he revealed Trace and Ellie's affair.

But if either of them had tried to hurt Jessie, he needed to push for answers.

She rubbed her temple with her fingers, and he choked back any more questions. She had had a rough night. She needed rest, not pressure.

"You need to get some sleep."

"I can't sleep yet," she whispered. "Will you sit and talk to me for a minute?"

Her eyes looked so soft, her body small and vulnerable, her voice beckoning him by her side. And he knew that she was independent and didn't ask for help often.

Unable to resist, he gave a short nod, and reclaimed the chair, bracing his legs apart. He ached to pull her hands into his again.

To connect with her and hold her and kiss her pain away.

"Tell me about your family," she said. "You grew up on the reservation?"

The last topic he wanted to discuss was his past. "Yes. My father still lives there."

"How about your mother?"

He chewed the inside of his cheek, then removed his Stetson and set it on the bedside table. "My mother committed suicide when I was a teenager after my younger brother's death."

Jessie's eyes filled with sympathy. Sympathy he didn't want.

Still, when she reached for his hand, he relented, clung to the scent of her skin.

"What happened?" she whispered.

A long-suffering sigh escaped him. "My mother was white, my father Comanche. People around town gave them a hard time, then my little brother became ill. My mother begged my father to take him to the hospital, but my father believes only in the old ways. He insisted on using the Big Medicine Ceremony to heal him instead."

"Oh, God," Jessie whispered. "I'm so sorry, Cabe."

Cabe shrugged. "So, you see, I think hospitals are good places to be when you're ill." This time he did reach up and touch her, just a gentle sweep of his fingers across her brow. "Or when you're injured."

"Do you still see your father?"

He shook his head. "We had a falling out when I decided to leave the reservation and Comanche Creek. Like some of the other Natives, he felt I was turning my back on him and the old ways."

"Were you?"

Her directness surprised him. "In a way, I guess I was," he admitted. "But my culture is still a part of me. I'm just not married to it to the point that I refute the advantages of modern ways."

"Your Native blood allowed you to sense the spirits on the land?"

A small smile curved his mouth. "Yeah."

"And the other Rangers brought you here because they thought you could bridge the gap between the two factions in town?"

He chuckled sarcastically. "I told them it was a mistake. I never fit into either group. In time, I thought things would change, but apparently they haven't."

"Not everyone shares those prejudices, Ranger." She reached up and pressed her hand against his cheek. A tingle ripped through him as her soft skin brushed his rough jaw. He'd seen so much violence on the job, so much hatred between the people, so much cruelty that her tenderness tripped emotions in his chest.

The sudden urge to hear her say his name slammed into him. The need to kiss her followed. "It's Cabe," he said in a low voice. "Call me Cabe."

A tiny smile curved her mouth, making her look

more beautiful than he could have imagined. "All right, Cabe. And just so you know, I think you *can* bridge the gap here, that you're exactly what this town needs."

He didn't believe her. But her voice sounded like an angel's.

Yet angelic thoughts fled when her damp tongue slipped out to trace her lips. He wanted his mouth there, wanted to taste her. Her breath hitched as if she recognized the hunger in his eyes.

He expected her to drop her hand, to tell him it was time for him to leave. Instead, she traced her fingers down to his mouth, scraping beard stubble in her path. She was so soft next to his rough exterior. So gentle, while he dealt with hard-core criminals and violence.

Even injured and weak, he'd never seen anything so beautiful.

"Cabe…"

"Tell me to go," he said, already bracing himself for her to utter the words.

"Please don't." Her breath whispered against his cheek as she gently coaxed his face toward her.

His body hardened, need firing through his sex, and he finally gave in to his need and claimed her mouth with his.

Chapter Eight

Cabe had never tasted anything as deliciously sweet as Jessie's kiss. Hungry for more, he traced the seam of her mouth with his tongue, probing her lips apart so he could delve inside. She moaned his name, and arousal splintered through him in shocking waves that threatened to destroy his sanity.

Sliding his hands through the silky tresses of her hair, he pulled her closer, angling her head so he could deepen the kiss. Heat flared between them as she flicked out her tongue to meet his. Their lips and tongues danced in a lover's dance, sweet, tender, erotic, passionate.

He wanted more. Wanted to touch her, trace her entire body with his fingers and his tongue. Wanted to strip her and climb in that bed and plant himself on top of her, inside her, wrap her up in his body. A body that was raging out of control with hunger and desire.

A knock sounded on the door, then the door squeaked open. "Um, excuse me."

Cabe tore himself away, then whirled his head around

to see the doctor standing in the doorway. He glanced back at Jessie, and saw her dazed look. She looked well-kissed, her hair tousled, her chest rising and falling with a labored breath.

A blush crept up her face, and even though he knew it was wrong, a smile of pleasure ripped through him.

"Miss Becker, I just came to check on you," the doctor said.

The realization that he'd crossed the line hit Cabe with gut-wrenching force, and he walked to the window, putting his back to Jessie while the doctor approached her bed.

Dammit, he was a Texas Ranger. A professional.

But he'd been kissing Jessie senseless, fantasizing about climbing in bed with her and making love to her when she was injured and in a damn hospital room. He'd really screwed up this time.

Jessie was a part of the task force, her family murder suspects, his ability to maintain control and objectivity vital to doing his job.

Sleeping with Jessie Becker could destroy that objectivity. Could mess with his head.

Distrust rose like a fireball in his belly. And what if she was just using him, seducing him so he wouldn't arrest her father?

JESSIE'S BODY TINGLED with need, the desires Cabe had stirred with that kiss making her ache for another round.

For more of his mouth on her. His lips touching hers.

But Cabe turned his back to her as the doctor approached, and she had to pull herself together.

"Hello, Miss. Becker. I'm Dr. Finwick. How are you doing?"

"I'm ready to go home."

The older man chuckled. "Tomorrow will be soon enough. You do have a minor concussion, but your X-rays and the CAT scan look good. You need to take it easy for a couple of days."

Jessie sighed. "All right, Doctor."

"Any nausea?"

Jessie shook her head. "No. I'm just tired."

"Then rest. But the nurse will come in to check on you periodically during the night."

The doctor glanced at Cabe, then her. "I'll see you in the morning, Miss Becker." The door closed behind him, and Jessie sighed.

"Cabe?"

His shoulders stiffened, but he refused to face her. "You heard the doctor. Get some sleep."

She lifted her fingers to her lips, aching for him again, missing the closeness. "Don't you want to talk about what happened?"

Finally he turned toward her, but the hunger and desire in his eyes had faded. Instead the brooding cop had resurfaced and distrust colored his expression. "It was just a kiss, a mistake," he said matter-of-factly. "Forget about it, Jessie. Nothing can happen between us."

His words were like a slap in the face.

He was here to investigate her family, and when the case ended, he would leave Comanche Creek. He'd already made it clear that he didn't belong here, and that he hadn't wanted to come back.

If offer card is missing write to: The Reader Service, P.O. Box 1867, Buffalo, NY 14240-1867, or visit www.readerservice.com

NO POSTAGE
NECESSARY
IF MAILED
IN THE
UNITED STATES

BUSINESS REPLY MAIL
FIRST-CLASS MAIL   PERMIT NO. 717   BUFFALO, NY

POSTAGE WILL BE PAID BY ADDRESSEE

THE READER SERVICE
PO BOX 1867
BUFFALO NY 14240-9952

Send For
2 FREE BOOKS
Today!

I accept your offer!

Please send me two free *Harlequin Intrigue®* novels and two mystery gifts (gifts worth about $10). I understand that these books are completely free—even the shipping and handling will be paid—and I am under no obligation to purchase anything, ever, as explained on the back of this card.

About how many NEW paperback fiction books have you purchased in the past 3 months?

❏ 0-2   ❏ 3-6   ❏ 7 or more
E4HM   **E4HX**   **E4JA**

❏ I prefer the regular-print edition   ❏ I prefer the larger-print edition
182/382 HDL   **199/399 HDL**

Please Print

FIRST NAME

LAST NAME

ADDRESS

APT.#   CITY

STATE/PROV.   ZIP/POSTAL CODE

Visit us online at
www.ReaderService.com

© 2009 HARLEQUIN ENTERPRISES LIMITED. ® and ™ are trademarks owned and used by the trademark owner and/or its licensee. Printed in the U.S.A.

▶ Detach card and mail today. No stamp needed.

H-I-03/10

And after hopping from one town to another all her life, she wanted and *needed* a home, a life and a family here in Comanche Creek.

CABE WAITED UNTIL JESSIE finally fell asleep, then settled in the chair to grab some shut-eye himself. He didn't trust that whoever had attacked her might not return to finish the job.

His mind ticked over the suspects. Trace topped the list. And then there was Ellie, her anger about the land deal, her political aspirations and her relationship with Trace.

She stirred in her sleep and whispered his name, and he had to clench the chair edge with his hands to keep from going to her.

She was growing more and more intriguing, more and more appealing.

More and more of a threat to his control and sanity.

But haunting memories of losing his mother and brother taunted him, and he forced any emotions aside.

He was a loner, and he liked it that way. No entanglements, no commitments.

Except to his badge.

Besides, Jonah Becker would probably kill him if he touched his daughter's lily-white skin with his dark hands.

Muttering a curse, he leaned back in the chair and closed his eyes. He'd grab a few winks before morning. Then he'd drive Jessie home, confront Jonah and take his blood and a DNA sample.

He also needed to visit Charla and get that list of artifacts and the buyers. Maybe the lab would have some results for him on the evidence he'd processed so far.

Finally sleep claimed him, but it was fitful. Every time Jessie moved or moaned, he woke and checked to make sure she was all right. And when she whispered his name in the middle of the night, he almost succumbed to temptation and crawled in bed with her.

They both might have slept better if he'd held her.

But he'd already traveled into dangerous territory with that heated kiss, and his willpower couldn't endure any more tests. At least not tonight.

The night dragged by, but as morning light cracked the sky, the nurses brought breakfast. He stepped outside for coffee and to call the lab. "Did you find out anything on the bullets I sent yesterday morning?"

"Yes, Sergeant, they came from a .38. Find the gun, and we can make a match."

"Right." Easier said than done, but he refused to give up. "I collected bullets from a shooting in town last night and they're being couriered over, along with two black hairs I found at the scene of an attack on Jessie Becker. Compare them to the strands found at the gravesite, and see if they match."

"I'll let you know as soon as I have time to process them."

"What about that clay sample used to glue the victims' eyes shut in the ritualistic burial? Did it match the clay from Jonah Becker's property?"

"Yes, sir. It's a match."

Cabe's lungs tightened. That wasn't good for Jessie's father.

Of course, he could argue that any number of people, including his hands, had access to the land.

"Thanks." He jammed some coins into the vending machine and watched as coffee spewed into a foam cup. Needing the caffeine buzz, he blew on the black coffee and took a sip. Steering his mind back to the case, he phoned Hardin and asked for a warrant to search the Becker house for a weapon.

"I'll have it when you stop by the office," Reed said. "The one for Becker's DNA sample and blood is on my desk."

"Thanks. I appreciate your assistance, Sheriff."

By the time he disconnected and reached Jessie's room, Jessie was signing release papers. "Now remember, take it easy," the doctor ordered. "Do you need me to call someone to drive you home?"

Cabe cleared his throat. "That's not necessary. I've got it covered."

Jessie shot him an almost panicked look. She knew he was going to interrogate her father. She'd been protective of him ever since the investigation started. Wyatt had speculated that she'd appointed herself Jonah's spokesperson to cover for him.

The doctor left the room, and Jessie pushed away the covers. "I need my clothes."

"Where are they?"

"In the cabinet." She swayed slightly, and he reached for her, but she threw up a warning hand. "I'm fine. I just stood up too quickly."

A stubborn look tightened her mouth as she shuffled over to the closet and dug out a plastic bag which held the clothes she'd been wearing when the medics brought her in.

"Do you need help?" he asked, then immediately regretted the question when she glared at him.

"No."

He offered her a clipped nod. "Fine. I'll wait outside." More for his own sanity than for her. If he saw her naked, he'd definitely lose his grip.

A minute later, the nurse appeared with a wheelchair, and he went to pull the SUV up to the hospital pick-up area.

"I could have called someone," Jessie said when he climbed out to help her into his vehicle.

Cabe cut her off. "Don't sweat it, Jessie. We're working together on this task force, and you've nearly been shot twice and then attacked. I don't intend to let you out of my sight until this case is over."

Shock strained her face. "What?"

He chuckled at the horror in her voice. "You heard me. I'm your bodyguard."

Even as he said the words, worry knotted his gut along with protective instincts—and arousal.

He sure as hell didn't want anything bad happening to her body. In fact, his hands and tongue itched to give her pleasure.

Jessie fastened her seat belt. "I can't believe this is happening."

Her sour tone reminded him that he'd hurt her by dismissing the kiss the night before. "I know you don't like it," he said. "All the more reason we figure out who attacked you, and who killed all these people and lock them up. Then you can go back to your life and your daddy."

"Like he really cares if I'm here," she muttered.

He turned to stare at her, confused by her statement. "I thought you and your father were close."

"And I thought you were tough and strong, not a coward, Cabe."

He gritted his teeth. "What the hell do you mean by that?"

"One hot, explosive kiss between us, and you run from me just like you ran from the town and your family."

A fireball of anger erupted in his gut. "You don't know what you're talking about."

"Don't I?" She crossed her arms and turned to look out the window. "But don't worry, I'd never beg a man for his affection."

He frowned, disturbed by her statement. Was she talking about him or her father?

It's none of your business, he reminded himself.

Jessie lapsed into silence as he swung by the sheriff's office to retrieve the warrants, and her mood grew more anxious as they approached the Double B.

The sight of the cattle grazing in the fields and the horses roaming in the pens stirred his baser love of the wild rugged land of Texas. He'd been so busy chasing his career and criminals the past few years that he'd forgotten how much he missed it.

Becker might be unscrupulous in his business tactics, but he ran a first-class operation, had always raised prime stock and was rumored to have incorporated the latest techniques to create leaner beef and treat his animals humanely.

Was he capable of murder?

JESSIE STRUGGLED TO ADOPT a congenial face as Cabe parked in front of the main house. The damn man was infuriating.

His dismissal the night before roused her insecurities. Her father had let her go with her mother because he hadn't loved her enough to fight for her. And since then, every relationship she'd had had failed. She knew that was her fault—she'd closed herself off from others, had guarded her heart.

So why was Cabe Navarro getting to her?

Reminding herself that she didn't *need* a man, or Cabe's affections, she forced her personal feelings aside. She had bigger problems to worry about.

So far, she'd been able to protect her father from the Rangers' interrogation tactics. But Cabe was persistent, and wouldn't give up.

What if he detected her father's mental capacity had diminished? Would Cabe take advantage of his condition? Make it public knowledge?

"Jessie, you know I have to get to the truth," Cabe said as they climbed out and walked up to the front entrance. "This is not personal."

Was he apologizing before the storm? "It is personal to me," she said quietly as she opened the door.

Lolita rushed toward her, her hands plastered to her cheeks, her eyes filled with concern. "Oh, my goodness, Miss Jessie, we have been so worried. Wilbur told us you were attacked. Your daddy is frantic."

Jessie's heart clenched. "I'm fine, Lolita." She gestured toward Cabe. "This is Ranger Sergeant Cabe Navarro. Where's Dad?"

Lolita's once-over was filled with disdain. "In his study. I tried to convince him to go back to bed, but he insisted he couldn't rest until he saw you."

"Thanks, Lolita. I'll go and assure him I'm fine."

Inhaling a deep breath, Jessie silently prayed her father was coherent as she crossed the foyer to his study. She felt Cabe's eyes boring into her back, and hoped she could pull off this meeting without any trouble.

Palms sweaty, she rapped on the door, then pushed it open. "Dad, it's me. And Ranger Sergeant Navarro is with me."

Her father pivoted his office chair toward her, then stood. Exhaustion lined his face along with worry. "My God, Jessie, Wilbur said you were attacked, that you were in the hospital."

"I'm sorry, Dad. I should have called, but it happened late last night and you were in bed. I'm fine, really."

He swept her into a hug, which made fresh tears swell in Jessie's eyes. It was the first time he'd shown affection toward her since she'd returned.

"I was so worried about you, baby." He pulled back to examine her. "What happened?"

Cabe cleared his throat. "Someone assaulted Jessie in the barn, sir. I recovered a hammer I believe her assailant used. Hopefully we can lift some trace from it and nail whoever did it."

Her father's gaze darted to Cabe and he released her. Deep groove lines fanned besides his mouth as he scowled. "I don't believe we've met."

Cabe extended his hand. "Ranger Navarro. I'm here investigating the recent murders."

Her father's forehead creased with a scowl. "And what exactly are you doing with my daughter?"

Jessie pressed a soothing hand to her father and urged him back to his chair. "Sergeant Navarro came out to the barn to investigate my attack last night, Dad. And he drove me home from the hospital."

"Why would someone want to hurt my daughter?" Jonah asked.

The tension thrumming through the room made Jessie's head throb again.

"I don't know, sir. Perhaps someone in town thinks she's covering for your crimes."

Jessie gasped at his bluntness. "Cabe—"

"We all know that the land you purchased was made through an illegal deal, Mr. Becker," Cabe continued. "And the most recent cadaver I found proves that that land is a Native American burial ground."

"I had no knowledge of a burial ground when I purchased that property. Billy Whitley faked those papers." Jonah rubbed a hand over his chin. "Why can't you let it go? That damn Whitley man wrote a confession before he killed himself."

Cabe cleared his throat. "We now believe that note was forged, Mr. Becker. That Billy didn't commit suicide, that he was murdered. And—" he paused, his gaze meeting Jessie's "—forensics proves that the clay used to glue the murder victims who were buried in the ritualistic style came from your property."

Jessie's arm tightened around her father's shoulders. "Anybody could have sneaked onto the ranch, dug up the soil and buried those bodies while we were all asleep. Someone is framing my father."

"Maybe," Cabe admitted. "All the more reason for me to continue this investigation." He removed the warrant from his rawhide jacket. "Sir, I have a warrant requesting a sample of your DNA and blood."

"Why my blood?" Jonah asked.

"Because the killer's blood was mixed in the face paint used on the bodies. If you are innocent, then letting me test your blood can eliminate you as a suspect."

Her father's strained expression sent alarm through Jessie. She hadn't been around her father in years. How well did she know him?

If he was innocent, why did he look so nervous?

Chapter Nine

Cabe took the DNA and blood sample and locked them in his crime kit. Then he left a disgruntled Jessie with her equally hostile father while he searched Trace's room for the .38. As he expected though, Trace's suite was clean.

The house furnishings had a country feel. Paintings of horses and the rugged land decorated the walls, antiques, oak and pine furniture filled the rooms, and handmade quilts covered the beds.

A room with a four-poster bed draped in pink satin drew his eye, the rosebud wallpaper suggesting it was Jessie's room. Or it had been in the past. The closet was bare of a woman's clothes, and there were no personal photos on the dresser or walls. He made a mental note to ask Jessie where she was sleeping. If not in the main house, she could be staying in one of the smaller cabins on the Double B.

On the chance that Trace had hidden the gun somewhere else in the house, he searched the upstairs quarters, the closets, drawers, then the downstairs suite which belonged to Jonah.

Inside Jonah's bathroom, he found several bottles of prescription pills, an array of vitamins, medication for high blood pressure, cholesterol, arthritis… Was the old man's health failing?

No gun anywhere in his room though, so he headed to the kitchen. The cook glared at him, and he asked her to step out of the room while he searched. The pantry was stocked with food, liquor and a variety of teas. He pushed the cans and boxes around, even checked the canister set in case Trace had ditched the gun inside, but found nothing. The drawers held cooking supplies but no gun either.

Frustrated, he moved to the outside of the house, checked the garage, the gardening shed, the trash. But his search yielded nothing.

By the time he returned to Jonah's study, Trace had joined Jessie and her father.

Animosity radiated from Trace. "Dad called and said you were searching for a gun."

Suspicion mounted in Cabe's chest. "You own a .38? Where is it, Trace?"

Trace gave him a smug smile. "I did. But I loaned it to Ellie a few months ago."

Ellie? Evidence was stacking up against her. "I guess I'll have to talk to her again then."

"It won't do you any good," Trace said snidely. "Ellie said the gun went missing over a month ago."

Cabe clamped his mouth tight. "Did she file a report?"

"Yeah, with the sheriff's office. You can check."

"I will," Cabe said. Then he directed his gaze to

Jessie. "I'm going to check out the burial sites and see if Dr. Jacobsen has made any new discoveries."

"I'll go with you," Jessie said.

Cabe frowned. "Are you sure you're up to that? The doctor ordered you to rest."

She folded her arms, her jaw set stubbornly. "I'll rest once I prove that you're wrong about my father, Ranger. I want my family's name cleared and you off the land as soon as possible."

Cabe gritted his teeth. So, it was back to calling him Ranger instead of Cabe. Damn.

Not that he could blame her. She probably felt violated now he'd searched her family home.

Still, his job demanded he explore every lead and suspect. Even if he had to hurt Jessie in the process.

"I'd like to stop by my cabin, shower and change clothes before we go to the site," Jessie said as they stepped back outside. "I can meet you out there."

Cabe grunted. "No. I told you, you're in my protective custody now. I'll make a call to the sheriff and verify that Ellie filed that report on the gun while I wait."

Anything to distract himself from the fact that Jessie would be stripping naked in the bathroom, and that he had to keep his hands off.

"YOU'RE NOT GOING to spend the night at my house," Jessie argued as Cabe drove her to the cabin she kept on the ranch.

Cabe shot her an impatient look. "Jessie, someone tried to kill you last night in the barn, and before that we were both shot at in town. I am staying with you, so get used to it."

She'd like to get used to it. That was the problem.

But having him in her home, near her things, leaving his scent and the imprint of his body behind would be pure torture.

Still, she refused to give him the satisfaction of revealing how much he rattled her. And how much she wanted a repeat of that kiss.

Instead, she muttered a sound of disgust and stared out the window, the sight of the horses running freely in the pasture a reminder that she was no longer free.

"Sounds more like prison," Jessie muttered.

"I'm sorry you feel that way," he said in a low voice. "But it's better than being dead."

Of course he was right. But she didn't have to like it.

A minute later, he parked at her cabin, then she jumped from his SUV and hurried to the door. She needed to escape Cabe's presence. He was confusing the hell out of her. Last night when she'd been injured, he'd been protective and tender. And when he'd shared the story about his family and his brother's death, she'd felt a connection, an intimacy that had roused deep feelings for the man.

He had obviously been caught between two worlds, two cultures, his entire life. And now to return and face the same issues and prejudices had to be difficult.

And that kiss…that kiss had been erotic and sensual and had incited a hunger in her body that only he could sate.

Damn the man.

But today he'd acted as if that kiss had never

happened. As if it had meant nothing. As if they were complete strangers.

He was back to professional cop mode—cold, distant, brooding. He could arrest her father and throw him in jail without hesitation—or concern for her.

Irritated with herself for wanting him anyway, she left him standing in her den, looking out of place next to her feminine décor and antiques.

Seething, she rushed to her bedroom and bath, then stripped her clothes, tossed them in the laundry basket, and climbed in the shower beneath the warm spray of water. The sharp pain in her temple had subsided into a dull ache, and exhaustion pulled at her. All she wanted to do was crawl in bed and sleep the day, and her worries, away.

Except she didn't want to crawl in bed alone. She wanted Cabe tucked in beside her, holding her, caressing her, running his fingers over her bare skin and making her body hum.

Closing her eyes, she imagined him opening the bathroom door, stripping and standing in the midst of the steamy small room. She could see his powerful muscles bunch on his arms, his broad chest rising and falling as he stared at her, his thick long length hardening and throbbing to be inside her.

Stop it, Jessie. You're not going to throw yourself at a man like your mother.

Especially not Cabe Navarro, the Texas Ranger who wants to put your father in jail.

Darn it. She rinsed, climbed out and dried off. While she'd been fantasizing about the man, he was probably snooping around her cabin looking for evidence to incriminate her family.

It was up to her to save her father.

And the only way she knew to do that was to help Cabe find out the truth about the murders.

Then he could leave town, and she could forget that she'd ever wanted him.

CABE PUNCHED IN the sheriff's number while he studied Jessie's house. Light pine furniture and earth tones dominated the connecting den and kitchen. An afghan embroidered with horses draped the top of a crème sofa, and candlewick throw pillows were scattered across the back. Splashes of soft green in the two wing-backed chairs and matted photos added color.

Interesting that she'd chosen to stay in this small place when the main house had enough room to accommodate her.

But she and Trace obviously didn't get along, so she probably needed the distance between them. God knew he couldn't stand the bastard.

Sheriff Hardin's voice came over the line, yanking him back to the case.

"Hardin, it's Navarro. Listen, I searched the Becker ranch house for that .38 but didn't find it. Trace admitted he owned one, but said he gave it to Ellie."

"Trace gave Ellie a gun?"

"Yeah. Apparently they've been having an affair."

"Geesh. That's news," Hardin muttered.

"Shocked me, too. And Jessie had no idea." The shower water kicked off, and Cabe inhaled a deep breath, forcing his mind off an image of Jessie's naked body. "Anyway, Trace claims that Ellie told him the gun went missing about a month ago. Did she file a report?"

"Not with me, but she might have filed it with one of my deputies. Let me check."

Papers rustled in the background, and Cabe walked over to the fireplace and studied the collection of iron horses Jessie had lined up on the mantel. Odd, but there were no family photos, no cozy shots of her and Jonah here either.

"Here it is," Hardin said, interrupting his thoughts. "It was dated six weeks ago. Shane Tolbert took the report."

"Tolbert. Funny how his name keeps cropping up."

Hardin made a clicking sound with his teeth. "I know, it is disturbing."

"So what was Ellie's story?" Cabe asked.

"According to the report, Ellie insisted the .38 was in her purse at one of the rallies. A fight broke out, and later she discovered it was missing."

"So any number of people could have stolen it."

"Yeah. Looks that way."

Another dead end. "I have the DNA and blood sample from Jonah Becker. I'm going to run by the burial sites and see if Dr. Jacobsen has found anything else, then talk to Charla Whitley and meet up with you later."

Jessie appeared in the doorway just as he ended the call. She'd swept her long curls into a ponytail, pulled on a hot-pink T-shirt and jeans, all of which should have made her look like a tomboy. But the pink shirt highlighted the natural rosy glow of her lips and cheeks. And the way the thin fabric hugged her breasts made his mouth water. Dragging his gaze from her chest, he forced his eyes south. But that proved no better. Those tight jeans showcased hips and lean muscular legs that he wanted wrapped around him.

Damn.

She jammed her Stetson on her head. "Ready?"

Cabe nodded, and they walked silently to his SUV, the midday sun heating his back and neck. Five minutes later, he parked at the site where they'd discovered the bodies. Crime scene tape still roped off the various areas, and Dr. Jacobsen had built a platform over the excavation site of the Native American graves to protect the grounds and bones.

A slight rumbling beneath Cabe alerted him to the disgruntled spirits below, the whisper of the spirits rising up to him from their graves and pleading for justice. War drums pounded, the screams of the dead piercing and painful.

A small handful of students had gathered to assist Dr. Jacobsen, who was running some kind of machine over the grounds. When she looked up and spotted him, she stopped, leaned it against an oak and approached them.

"What are you doing?" Cabe asked.

Nina tilted the brim of her cap, squinting through the sun. "Using ground penetrating radar—it's called GSSI, Subsurface Interface Radar—to search for other graves. The equipment can detect coffins as well as bones buried beneath the ground."

Cabe scoured the land visually, wondering how many bodies might actually be buried here. "Have you found any other burial spots?"

An excited smile spread over her face. "I sure have. Two so far, but there are more, I just know it."

Jessie's brow furrowed. "You found two more. My God."

Nina motioned for them to follow her. "I also unearthed two more artifacts which confirm our theory about the bodies being Natives. Come and see."

Cabe and Jessie trailed her to a workstation she'd created beneath a tarp, and she indicated two items bagged and lying on the folding table.

Cabe's breath stilled in his chest. A gold armband adorned with garnets and Native American etchings—rare and probably priceless. And a pacho, a prayer stick, notched out of painted cottonwood.

"Those are beautiful," Jessie whispered.

"And extremely valuable," Nina added. "I also researched that headdress you found, Cabe, and confirmed that it was dated back to the 1700s."

Cabe whistled. "You're right. Collectors would pay a fortune for these as well as that headdress."

"My father didn't know anything about this," Jessie said defensively. "He wanted ranch land, not Native American artifacts."

But that antiquities broker, and Billy and Charla Whitley, had known, and they'd probably realized they had a treasure chest at their fingertips.

And if someone intended to expose the truth and stop their treasure hunting, any one of them might have killed to protect their secret fortune.

As Cabe drove toward Charla Whitley's house, Jessie twisted her hands in her lap.

She had to accept that the land her father purchased was a Native American burial site, and that it rightfully belonged to the Comanche people. Perspiration beaded on her neck, making her hair stick to her skin.

The only question in her mind was if her father had known that he'd bought it illegally. She wanted to protect him, but if he had knowingly cheated and robbed the Natives, her respect for him would be crushed.

Her cell phone jangled from her purse, and she grabbed it and connected the call. "Hello."

"This is Dr. Taber. May I speak to Miss Becker?"

Jessie's heart thumped. "This is Jessie."

"Miss Becker. I'm sorry to disturb you, but I wanted to touch base. I examined your father yesterday, and I hate to say it, but his mental capacity and coherency seems to be declining even more."

Worry knotted Jessie's stomach. She wanted good news. "What do you think is going on, Doctor?"

"I'm not sure. We'll probably need to run another battery of tests. I've consulted a specialist, and I'll be back in touch to schedule them. Meanwhile, maintain his medicine regime."

"Thanks, I will." Jessie hung up, feeling defeated, her heart heavy. She'd come home to reconnect with her father and now might lose him to prison, or possibly some physical disease. Life so wasn't fair.

Cabe pulled in front of Charla's sprawling ranch house, and she frowned as they made their way up the limestone walkway. Had Charla and Billy both known the truth about the burial grounds and tricked her father?

It was common knowledge that Charla collected Native American artifacts—had she sold them knowing they belonged to the Comanche Nation?

If so, she understood why the Comanche faction was so upset.

"What will happen to the artifacts you recover?" Jessie asked.

Cabe cleared his throat, then pressed the doorbell. "They'll be returned to the Comanche Nation."

Dark storm clouds hovered above, casting a gray to the sky, and the wind sent the mesquite beside the house bristling. A second later, Charla opened the door, clad in a bright purple gauzy blouse with Indian beading, a denim skirt and dozens of silver bracelets.

"We need to talk," Cabe said without preamble.

Charla's laser-sharp eyes cut over them, but she stepped sideways and gestured for them to enter. Jessie had never been in Charla's house and was surprised to find eclectic furnishings mixed with Native American blankets, leather containers and conches. Several shadowboxes contained handmade Native American jewelry, arrowheads, and one held an elaborate feather chest plate.

"I need those documents that we discussed and the name of the person or persons who bought the artifacts from you," Cabe said.

Charla sauntered over to an oak desk, removed a folder and handed it to Cabe. "As you requested, Ranger Navarro."

Cabe accepted the folder with a scrutinizing look. "We found more artifacts and bodies on the land," Cabe said. "Did you know about them, Charla?"

For a brief second, interest flickered in her eyes, before she masked it. "No."

"You're lying. I think you and Billy both knew," Cabe said. "And when Marcie realized what you planned to do, that you'd found a gold mine, you killed her and that broker to keep the artifacts to yourself. And everyone knows you hated Daniel Taabe." His voice hardened in disgust. "I just can't believe that you let Billy take the fall."

"You're wrong," Charla screeched. "And unless you have proof, which you obviously don't," Charla snapped, "get out."

"I'll get proof," Cabe warned. "And when I do, Charla, you're going to jail."

Fear flashed in Charla's eyes along with hatred. Cabe ignored her mutinous expression, then pivoted to leave.

Jessie followed, her heart thumping wildly. She'd never cared for Charla, but she'd also never thought her capable of murder. But today she'd witnessed a different side of the woman.

A dangerous side that made her wonder if Cabe was right. If Charla was a killer.

CABE REVIEWED THE documents Charla had given him, then the address for the buyer of the artifacts.

"What does it say?" Jessie asked.

"Charla sold them to a man named Mauri Mc-Landon. He lives in Austin." He started the engine and veered onto the highway. "We'll pay him a visit, then I'll drop the evidence in my crime kit at the lab."

Jessie's expression grew pinched, and he knew she was worried about the blood and DNA from her father. The urge to soothe her hit him, but he kept his hands firmly clamped around the steering wheel.

Still, for her sake, he hoped that the evidence exonerated the man.

Forty minutes later, he steered the SUV onto a sprawling piece of property outside of Austin, not a working ranch but a mansion set on fifty acres of prime real estate. Cabe made a quick mental assessment.

McLandon must have a fortune, and was a perfect buyer for Charla. She'd probably expected a hefty cash flow rolling in from the man.

Did McLandon know the artifacts belonged to the Comanches? Did he know about the murders, and if so, had he taken part?

He stopped at the security gate, and punched the button. "Ranger Sergeant Cabe Navarro," he said into the speaker. "I'm here to see Mr. McLandon."

A male voice answered. "Mr. McLandon isn't here right now."

Cabe hissed in frustration. "Can you tell me where he is? It's important I speak with him."

"He left a while ago."

"Does he have an office?"

"Yes, but he's not at the office. I believe he had a business lunch meeting."

"Then give me his cell phone number."

"I'm sorry, sir, but I'm not at liberty—"

"This is a police matter, sir," Cabe cut in bluntly. "Either give it to me, or I'll park myself in the house until he returns."

The security guard sighed loudly, then recited the number. Cabe punched it into his cell phone, but the phone clicked over to voice mail, so he left a message.

"Let's drop by the crime lab, then grab something to eat," Cabe suggested. "Maybe by then, McLandon will have returned my call."

Jessie nodded, and he swung the SUV around and headed back toward Austin. The land was isolated, flat, prime pastureland. In the distance, he spotted some wild mustangs racing across the prairie.

They were beautiful. Big, black horses galloping across the land—free.

He understood that need for freedom.

So why was the woman sitting next to him tempting him to throw aside his own freedom, drag her in his arms and bond with her?

Dark clouds opened up to dump rain on them, and he turned on the wipers and defroster and slowed.

But a truck raced up on his tail, forcing him to speed up. He squinted through the rain to discern the make and color, but only a small swatch of white flashed through the downpour.

Suddenly the trucker behind him gunned the engine, sped up and rammed into him.

Jessie screamed, her hand hitting the dashboard as the impact bounced her forward.

"Son of a bitch." Cabe clenched the steering wheel

in a white-knuckled grip in an attempt to keep the SUV on the road.

But a gunshot pinged the back windshield, then the truck slammed into his bumper again, and sent them careening off the embankment into the ditch.

Chapter Ten

Jessie screamed as the SUV bounced over the ruts and nosedived into a ditch. Tires screeched, metal crunched, and glass shattered.

She covered her head with her arms as the air bag exploded.

Cabe cursed, slashed his air bag, then hers, deflating them. "Are you okay, Jessie?"

"Yes...I think so."

A gunshot pinged off the vehicle from the bank above, and Cabe shoved his door open. "Stay down!"

He vaulted from the driver's seat, crouched down and circled behind the vehicle heading up the rugged slope. Jessie's pulse raced. Once again, she felt like a sitting duck with her life in Cabe's hands.

But another shot shattered the front windshield, and Jessie plastered herself on the seat face down.

Good heavens. Who was shooting at them?

Not her father—he'd never do anything to endanger her life. Besides, since his illness, he'd barely left the house.

But Charla had been irate and belligerent when they'd left her place. Had she followed them and tried to kill them?

CABE WAS SICK OF THIS cat-and-mouse game. He yanked his gun from inside his jacket, jogged up the hill and spotted the tail of a white truck roaring away. He fired at the tires, but the truck was too fast. It disappeared around the curve and into the distance spewing dust and rocks.

Dammit.

His mind ticked back to the details Wyatt and Reed and Livvy had gathered so far. Three people in Comanche Creek owned white pickups. Jonah, Ellie and Charla.

Considering the fact that they'd just left Charla's, she jumped to the top of his suspect list.

Remembering Jessie and the evidence he'd stored in his SUV, he jogged back down the hill. Rocks skidded beneath his rawhide boots as he approached the vehicle. If Charla had fired at them and run them off the road, she wouldn't get away with it.

His front bumper was jammed into the ditch, the rear end crunched from the impact of the truck. A small streak of white paint marred the back bumper.

Relief surged through him.

He'd have forensics process the paint sample—then he'd know who'd been driving that damn truck.

Heaving a breath, he spotted Jessie hunched over in the front seat. The air bag lay in shambles, glass littering the seat and floor. Jessie must have heard him because she jerked up her head.

Her beautiful eyes were wide and frightened, and a sliver of glass had caught in her hair.

Furious that she might have been injured, he stowed his weapon in his holster, then opened the door, knelt and plucked the glass fragment from her hair.

"Are you okay?" he asked gruffly.

She nodded. "Yes."

In spite of her reply, her voice quivered, and she was trembling. Needing to know she was safe as badly as she needed comfort, he pulled her into his arms. A sigh of relief gushed from her, and she fell against him. Breathing in the scent of her hair calmed him slightly, and she clung to him and buried her head against his chest as he stroked her back.

They held each other for what seemed like hours, him simply drinking in her sweetness. When she finally lifted her chin and looked into his eyes, the fear and vulnerability in her expression twisted his stomach into a fisted knot.

Adrenaline still churned through him, but hunger for her erupted like a flame that had just been lit.

To hell with keeping his distance. They'd damn near been killed. His control snapped, and he lowered his mouth and fused his lips with hers.

The low throaty moan she emitted sent a surge of raw need through him, and he deepened the kiss. She tasted delicious, like sweet tenderness and tenacity and a breath of sensuality. Her tongue reached out to tease him, and his chest heaved as he plunged into her mouth and made love to her with his tongue.

His hands dove into her hair, her hands clawing at his arms, and his jacket as if she wanted to strip him. He'd known she'd be a tigress in bed, and the thought of taking her right here in the car made his sex throb and harden.

But the sound of traffic above echoed. For God's sake, he was a law officer, and anyone who noticed that they'd crashed might see them. He couldn't do that to Jessie.

Forcing himself to end the kiss, he pulled away slightly and cupped her face between his hands. They were both breathing raggedly. "We need to go."

She nodded against him. "I know." Yet she didn't release him. Instead she tightened her hands on his chest. "Cabe, my father didn't run us off the road."

His dark eyes studied her. "How can you be sure?"

"Because he wouldn't shoot at me or a cop. He's too smart for that."

"Trace could have taken his truck," Cabe suggested.

"That's possible, but we just left Charla's. She probably called McLandon and warned him we were coming, then she chased us down."

"That's logical," Cabe said. "The truck left paint on my bumper. The lab should be able to identify the make and model. Then we'll pinpoint exactly whose truck hit us."

She slowly dropped her hands from his shirt, although an instant of regret flickered in her eyes. That made him want her even more.

"Then let's go," Jessie said, her voice stronger now. "Whoever murdered those people and cheated my father needs to pay."

CABE RAKED GLASS from his seat, then started the engine. It took several tries before he managed to extract the SUV from the ditch, but finally they bounced back onto the road. While he headed toward Austin, he phoned the sheriff and relayed the situation. "A white pickup truck slammed into us, ran us off the road and shot at us," he told Hardin. "We had just left Charla's. Check and see if she's home. If she is, look for evidence on her truck, maybe a dent or paint scratches."

Hardin mumbled agreement. "I'll drive to her place right now."

"Thanks." Cabe snapped his phone closed and glanced at Jessie. She sat huddled in the seat, her hair blowing from the wind flowing through the shattered window. Still, she didn't complain.

"What are you going to do about your SUV?" Jessie asked.

"While the lab processes it, I'll arrange for a rental."

She shivered and picked another piece of glass from the seat. "I still can't believe Charla tried to kill us."

Cabe had seen worse, but refrained from sharing. "Greed drives people to do unspeakable things."

Jessie lapsed into silence again, and when they arrived at the crime lab, he left her in the front office while he carried the evidence inside.

Gary Levinson, one of the CSI techs, took Jonah Becker's blood and DNA sample, while another tech rushed outside to the SUV to collect the paint sample.

Levinson led Cabe back to his workstation. "I analyzed those two black hairs you brought in from the burial sites."

"Did they match Ellie Penateka's?"

"No. As a matter of fact, the hair was naturally blond, but had been dyed."

Cabe considered that information, but no one specific came to mind.

"The DNA will take time to run, but the preliminary blood test will only take a few minutes."

"Good," Cabe said. Then he'd know if the blood used in the ritual burials matched Jonah's.

"I'm going to arrange for a rental truck while you run the test."

Levinson agreed, and Cabe stepped back into the front lobby and phoned Wyatt to give him an update. "The hairs I found at the burial site don't match Ellie Penateka's. In fact, the strands were naturally blond."

"Hmm, that could be helpful."

"Maybe. See what you can dig up on a man named Mauri McLandon," Cabe said. "According to the papers Charla gave me, he purchased the illegal artifacts from her."

"Hang on and I'll run him through the system," Wyatt said.

Cabe glanced around for Jessie and noticed her deep in conversation on the phone, her brows furrowed with worry.

"Listen, Dad, we'll talk about it when I get home," she said softly. "Please don't upset yourself."

She cast Cabe a wary look, then walked to the corner to speak in private.

"Navarro," Wyatt said, jerking him back to the conversation. "I found McLandon. He's five-eleven, has short brown hair, hazel eyes, weighs about 180. He's an independent dealer with a long line of family money, and lives in Austin."

"Yeah, I know. I went to his house but he wasn't home, and I've left a message on his cell. Does he have a record?"

"He was arrested a couple of years ago for selling a fake painting, but he beat the charges. Claimed he had no idea the painting was a forgery, that someone must have replaced the one he bought with a forged one."

"Call the Austin police and see if they can pick him up for questioning. We need to get the artifacts he bought from Charla back."

"Will do." He ended the call and approached Jessie. She looked exhausted, her hair disheveled, her face showing signs of strain. Judging from the fact that she'd been attacked the night before, suffered a head injury and had nearly died today, she had a right to look frayed.

But he sensed something else was bothering her. Something to do with her father. What was she hiding?

She ran a hand through her hair, then tucked a strand behind her ear. She looked so damn vulnerable that he wanted to drag her in his arms and comfort her again.

Considering they were in the lab and the CSI was processing her father's blood, though, he resisted.

"What's happening?" she asked.

"Let's pick up the rental and grab something to eat while CSI processes my truck and the evidence I brought in."

"They're testing my father's blood?"

He met her gaze, his chest tightening slightly at the apprehension in her eyes. "Yes."

Her face paled slightly, but she pasted on a forced smile of bravado, then followed him outside. They took a cab to the rental agency, rented a Jeep, then found a Mexican cantina in downtown Austin. Jessie nibbled at her burrito while he inhaled a platter of fajitas. He knew she was worried about the test results and couldn't blame her.

If the blood matched Jonah's, he'd have proof that her father was a cold-blooded killer. And he'd have to arrest him.

JESSIE PUSHED AWAY from the table, unable to eat for her churning stomach. Her father had been irate about undergoing more tests.

There had also been trouble on the ranch. Some fencing had been intentionally cut, allowing several head of cattle to escape. The stream in the north pasture had completely dried up, so they needed to move the cattle to another pasture, or reroute water, which would be costly.

The waitress brought the bill, and she reached for it, but Cabe snatched it. "I'll pay."

"We can split it," Jessie offered.

Cabe glared at her. "I said I'd take care of it."

"Fine." Needing a reprieve from him before she broke down, she excused herself and went to the ladies' room while he paid the bill. Nerves knotted her muscles as they drove back to the crime lab.

The CSI tech Cabe introduced as Levinson met them in the front office.

"What are the results?" Cabe asked.

The CSI tech flipped open the folder in his hands. "The blood type did not match Jonah Becker's. He's O negative, the blood from the clay is A positive."

Jessie nearly staggered with relief. "I knew it wouldn't."

"How about the paint sample?" Cabe asked.

"My guy is still working on that. He's running a program to trace the type of paint with the make and model of the vehicle now. I'll call you when he pinpoints the information."

Cabe thanked him, then they walked back outside to the Jeep. The earlier downpour had dwindled to a light rain, the sound almost calming as it drummed on the roof of the car.

"Have you checked Charla's blood?" Jessie asked.

"Not yet, but I intend to." Cabe gave her a sideways glance as he shifted gears and wove into traffic. "What's wrong with your father, Jessie?"

"I don't want to discuss my father with you." Night had fallen, the storm clouds obliterating the moon and casting a grayness across the rugged land as they left the city.

"I'm not the enemy," Cabe said gruffly. "And for what it's worth, I'm glad the blood didn't match your father's. I don't want to see you hurt."

Jessie rubbed her arms with her hands to ward off a sudden chill. "Come on, Cabe. You don't like my father. You wanted him to be guilty."

Cabe's hands tightened around the steering wheel. "That's not true, Jessie. All I want is to find the person or persons responsible for these murders."

Regret slammed into Jessie for her accusation. Cabe had faced prejudices his entire life, and had good reason to have been suspicious of her father.

She wanted to reach out and soothe his jaw, apologize, confess that she admired his dedication to his job. That she actually liked and admired *him*.

And that she yearned for him to kiss her again. Spend the night in his arms. And maybe longer.

But he would be leaving soon, and if she allowed herself to succumb to her feelings, she was terrified she'd lose her heart to him.

And Jessie Becker didn't give her heart to anyone.

JESSIE SHOULD HAVE been relieved her father's blood hadn't matched the killer's, but the fact that she still seemed agitated worried Cabe. There was obviously more to the problems with her father than she wanted to admit.

He remembered the number of pill bottles in Jonah's medicine cabinet and frowned. Just how sick was the man? Was that the real reason Jessie had moved back to the ranch? To take care of Jonah?

His cell phone trilled, and he grabbed it. "Navarro."

"It's Hardin. I went by Charla's house, but she wasn't home so I posted a deputy to watch the house in case she returns."

"Good. I need a warrant for a sample of her blood. Jonah Becker's was not a match. CSI is still working on the paint sample they extracted from my SUV." He glanced at Jessie, and saw her rub her temple. "And Lieutenant Colter is calling the Austin police to pick up McLandon, the man who purchased the artifacts from Charla."

"Thanks for the update," Hardin said. "I'll let you know if Charla turns up."

Cabe snapped his phone closed and glanced at Jessie again. "You look exhausted," he said as they neared the Becker property. "I'll drive you straight to your cabin."

"No, I want to stop by the main house and check on my father."

The rain had died as he pulled through the turnstile gate, drove up the winding drive and parked in front of the main ranch house. Cabe climbed out and followed Jessie inside. Lolita greeted her and asked if she wanted dinner.

"No, thanks, I ate," Jessie said. "I just want to check on Dad."

"He's in the study," Lolita said, then clucked her mouth sadly. "But I'm afraid he's had a bad day."

Jessie thanked the woman, then crossed the foyer to the study, rolling her shoulders as if to prepare for trouble.

As soon as she opened the door, Jonah's ranting echoed from within. Cabe stopped at the doorway to give her privacy, but the man's chalky pallor and wild-eyed look shocked him. Jonah seemed disoriented and confused, a different man from the one he'd spoken with earlier.

"Rachael, don't leave me again," Jonah cried. "Please don't go."

"It's Jessie, Daddy," she said softly. "Calm down. Everything's going to be all right. I promise."

Sympathy for Jessie shot through Cabe. Jonah must be suffering from dementia or some other mental incapacity. That was the reason Jessie had been covering for him. It also meant that someone could have duped him into the illegal land deal without him being aware the documents were forged.

Cabe had the sudden urge to shoulder her burdens. But he didn't want to violate her privacy. Still, standing outside the door and listening as the man continued to rant incoherently and she attempted to calm him took every ounce of his willpower.

Meanwhile Lolita walked in with tea and a tray with pills on it.

Cabe's impatience mounted as the minutes ticked by, but finally Lolita and Jessie came through the door, flanking Jonah on both sides as they coaxed him upstairs to bed.

"I want my nightcap," Jonah mumbled.

"Daddy, you don't need alcohol on top of your medication," Jessie said.

"But Trace always gives it to me," Jonah said in a petulant voice.

"Miss Jessie's right," Lolita agreed. "Mr. Jonah, you need to go to sleep."

Cabe turned away, then paced the foyer, anxious for Jessie to return. When she finally reappeared, fatigue lined her face and her eyes looked bloodshot from crying.

Dammit, he wanted to pull her in his arms and hold her. "Come on," he said softly. "You're going home and to bed yourself."

The fact that she didn't argue indicated the depth of her turmoil, and they rode to her cabin in silence.

Her shoulders sagged as they walked up to the cabin, and she unlocked the door. But she turned to him and stopped him from entering. "Cabe, you can go now. I'm home. I'll be fine."

He stepped inside and flipped on the light. "We've discussed this, and I'm not leaving." He gently took her shoulders. "I'm sorry about your father, Jessie. What do the doctors say?"

Her lip quivered. "They've run tests but haven't found anything definitive. And he seems to be getting worse." Her voice trailed off, and a tear rolled down her cheek.

Cabe clenched his jaw, but his heart ached for her and he pulled her into his arms. She collapsed against him, her body trembling as she struggled to suppress her tears.

Hating to see her suffer, he stroked her hair. "It's all right, Jessie. Just let it all out."

"No," she said, shaking her head. "I can't. I have to be strong for Dad's sake. He's counting on me."

A low chuckle rumbled from him. "You are strong, but you've been injured, shot at and nearly killed. All that and your father's illness, and I'm amazed you haven't fallen apart sooner."

"I don't want to fall apart."

"I know. But you can lean on me, and I won't tell anyone," he said in a teasing tone.

"No, I have to stand on my own." She clutched his arms. "And I have to protect Daddy. If word leaks that he's ill, business investors may refuse to work with us. And even you thought he was guilty of murder."

"Maybe if you'd confided to me about his condition, I would have dismissed him as a suspect earlier."

Her labored breath rattled in the air between them. "I know. But I wanted to protect him. To make him proud… I wanted him to love me."

Her last words wrenched his heart. Emotions churning in his throat, he swallowed to make his voice work. "How could he not love you, Jessie? You're beautiful, strong, smart, you take care of everyone, and you've helped make the ranch a success."

"Then why didn't he want me enough to fight for me years ago?" she whispered. "Why didn't he ever send for me or plan visits?"

Her anguish tore at him, and he had to alleviate her pain. So he lifted her chin, and forced her to look at him. "Ahh, Jessie…"

She tried to look away, seemed embarrassed that she'd admitted a weakness, which only fueled his admiration, and his need to assure her that she was loveable.

And that he wanted her.

Heat speared his body as her gaze met his and passion flared between them. Her feminine scent enveloped him, her eyes implored him to touch her, her lips begged for a kiss.

The pull of passion overcame him, and he succumbed to the need, lowered his head and claimed her mouth with his. She leaned into him, pressed her palm against his cheek, and met his kiss with a moan of desire.

Their tongues teased, danced together in a sensual rhythm that made hunger drive him to slide his hands down her shoulders, then to yank her up against him. She threaded her fingers into his hair, deepening the kiss and stroking his calf with her foot.

A groan of excitement erupted from deep in his chest, driving him to trail kisses along her jaw down to her neck. Hungry for more, he nibbled the sensitive flesh of her ear, then slipped open the buttons of her blouse to reveal luscious breasts encased in red lace.

God, she was sexy. All feminine and needy and whispering erotic sounds that made his sex throb.

With a flick of his fingers, he opened the front clasp of her bra, then hissed a breath of appreciation as her gorgeous breasts spilled from the restraints into his waiting hands.

She threw her head back in abandon, and he accepted her offering, and lowered his mouth to one ripe, bronzed nipple. She groaned and whispered his name, and he licked the tip of the turgid peak, teasing one breast then the other, until her breathing grew raspy.

His heart pounded with the need to take her, fast and furious, but he forced himself to slow down. He wanted to pleasure her, to alleviate her pain for the night.

Dammit, he wanted to forget the case existed, and show her that she could be loved.

That he wasn't the enemy, but a man who craved her body. One who'd wanted her from the moment he'd laid eyes on that fiery red hair and those killer legs.

He sucked her nipple between his lips, and her legs buckled. She clung to him as he lifted her and carried her to her bedroom. With one quick swipe, he tossed the homemade quilt back and laid her on the covers.

His body was wired, tense, his sex hard and aching, about to explode.

But just as he reached for the zipper to her jeans, a boom exploded in the distance.

Jessie stared at him in fear and horror. "That's in the north pasture," she whispered.

Cabe choked back a command to urge her to forget the noise, that he had to have her now, that he wanted to taste the sweet heart of her between her thighs and pound himself inside her until she cried out his name in ecstasy.

But the ground was rumbling, the echo of the explosion reverberating through the room.

They had to go.

PANIC SPURNED JESSIE into action. An explosion had occurred on her ranch. Were animals hurt? Work hands?

Cabe adjusted his jeans, and she realized his erection was still straining against his fly. For a brief second, she allowed herself to revel in the fact that he'd wanted her, and regretted the intrusion.

But the echo of that explosion haunted her. They had to find out what had happened.

"Ready?" Cabe asked.

She nodded, and they rushed outside to the Jeep. Her pulse raced as he sped over the ruts in the dirt road toward the northern end of the land. In the distance, she spotted smoke and dust curling into the darkness, and she prayed none of their hands had been injured.

"What the hell?" Cabe muttered as he threw the Jeep into Park.

Dirt and rock had been disturbed, bushes and small brush uprooted, a mound of broken rock blocking the creek. He removed his weapon and forced Jessie behind him as they climbed out and slowly searched the area.

"The creek in the upper part of north pasture has dried up," Jessie said. "Someone has been sabotaging us."

"No one is here," Cabe said as he swept a flashlight

across the terrain. "The explosion must have been set on a timer." He hissed, then swung around to Jessie. "The burial site. Whoever set this knew we'd come here to check it out. It was a diversion."

Jessie's pulse clamored with the realization that he was probably right, and they raced back to the Jeep, jumped in and flew to the site. As soon as they arrived, they leaped from the vehicle.

"Oh, my God," Jessie gasped, then pointed to a jagged rock. "There's Deputy Spears. He's been hurt."

Cabe pulled his gun again, his gaze skimming the perimeter as he crept toward the deputy, then knelt and checked for a pulse.

"Is he still alive?" Jessie whispered.

"Yes. Go back to the Jeep, call an ambulance and the sheriff."

Jessie's heart pounded as she raced to do as he said. But when she reached for the Jeep door, footsteps crackled behind her.

Then the cock of a gun echoed in the eerie silence.

Fear crawled up her spine, and she started to scream, but the sharp jab of a gun stabbing her back forced her into silence.

Chapter Eleven

Deputy Spears was still alive, but Cabe spotted another man lying on the ground beside the platform Nina had built, and cursed.

Blood oozed from his chest, and his eyes stared blankly into the night, wide with the shock of death. Judging from the description he'd been given of Mc-Landon, he guessed this was the collector who'd bought the artifacts from Charla.

A shuffling noise behind him made him twist around and swing his Sig up, ready to fire. But the blood rushed to his head when he spotted Charla pointing a gun at Jessie's head. Charla looked panicked, wild-eyed. Dangerous.

"Charla," he said between clenched teeth, "what are you doing?"

Her hand shook as she waved the .38 at Jessie's temple. "Make a move and I'll kill her."

"Charla, please don't do this," Jessie whispered. "No one else needs to die."

Charla shoved Jessie down onto her knees in the dirt.

"You should have left things alone," Charla cried. "None of this would have happened if you Rangers hadn't shown up. You've ruined everything."

"McLandon is dead," Cabe said. "Why did you kill him, Charla? Was he getting greedy?"

"Yes, the stupid jerk," she screeched. "He found out there were other artifacts here and got impatient."

"So he set that explosion to draw us away long enough for him to steal some of them," Jessie said.

"Yes," Charla wailed. "I tried to convince him it was too risky, to wait until things died down. But he wouldn't listen."

"So you shot him," Cabe said matter-of-factly.

Charla's face crumpled, tears blurring her eyes. "We fought and the gun went off. It was an accident." She snatched a hank of Jessie's hair and Jessie winced in pain.

"But it won't be an accident if you kill Jessie and me," Cabe said.

"Please, Charla," Jessie said. "We'll tell everyone you didn't mean to kill him."

"Was Billy's death an accident, too, Charla?" Cabe said harshly. "Or did you kill him because he threatened to expose you?"

"I didn't kill Billy," Charla shouted. "I would never have hurt him."

"But you doctored the papers for the land deal, then arranged the deal with Jonah."

A brittle laugh resounded from Charla. "Yes, and we made a good deal. He got the land and I got the artifacts."

"You took advantage of my father," Jessie shouted.

"Do you know how valuable those artifacts are?" Charla screamed. "They're worth a fortune."

"Yes, they're invaluable," Cabe said between gritted teeth. "But those artifacts belong to the Comanche Nation."

Charla shook her head madly. "Why? So they can sit in some stupid museum?"

"Is that why you killed that antiquities broker, Mason Lattimer?" Cabe asked. "And Ray Phillips? They discovered you didn't rightfully own those artifacts, and threatened to overturn the deal."

"Those stupid men panicked," Charla snapped. "They claimed there were spirits on the land, that they had been haunting them, that we had to return the artifacts."

"So you lured them out here, then murdered them and buried them in a ritualistic style to throw off the police and make them think that Daniel Taabe had killed them," Cabe said. "That's cold, premeditated murder, Charla."

Jessie twisted her head around to glare at Charla. "My father was sick, and you made the Rangers suspect him. How could you put him through that, Charla?"

"Shut up!" Perspiration trickled down Charla's face, and she raised the hand holding the gun and swiped her hair back from her face. "You should have stayed out of it, Jessie."

"And you shouldn't have murdered those innocent people!" Jessie snapped.

Cabe's finger tightened on his trigger, ready to fire, but Jessie swung her body around and jabbed her elbow into Charla's knee.

Charla yelped in pain, her leg buckling. She grappled

for control, but her gun fired into the air, and she fell backward and dropped the gun.

Cabe lunged forward in attack, and kicked the weapon out of reach. Charla struggled to push herself up, but Jessie punched her in the face, and she cried out as blood spurted from her nose.

Screeching like a crazed person, Charla launched up to attack Jessie, but Cabe aimed his gun at her chest. "It's over, Charla. Touch her and I'll shoot."

Charla froze, and he helped Jessie stand, keeping his Sig trained on Charla. The realization that she'd been caught registered in her defeated look, then she began to sob pathetically.

CHARLA LOOKED SO pathetic that Jessie almost felt sorry for her. But she had almost killed her, and she had committed multiple murders.

Sheriff Hardin roared up with Dr. McGrath, the coroner, on his tail, and an ambulance.

Cabe pushed Charla toward the sheriff's car while the paramedics rushed to take care of Deputy Spears.

"Charla tried to kill Jessie, and she confessed to murdering Lattimer, Phillips and McLandon," Cabe said.

Charla balked against the handcuffs, but Cabe squeezed her arm tightly. "There's no use fighting it, Charla. We caught you red-handed. You're going to jail for a long time."

"What about Marcie and Daniel Taabe?" the sheriff asked. "Did you kill them, too?"

"No," Charla cried. "I swear I didn't."

Jessie frowned. Why would she deny murdering two

other people when she was already going to jail for four counts of murder?

"Get in the car." Cabe shoved Charla's head down until she relented and collapsed in the backseat of the squad car. When the door slammed shut, pinning her in, she started to cry hysterically again.

Cabe shook his head in disgust, then turned to the sheriff. "McLandon, the man who bought the artifacts from Charla, is over there. He was shot in the chest. Charla claims it was an accident, that they fought for the gun and it went off."

The coroner nodded. "I'll do an autopsy." He headed over to examine the body. Cabe bagged Charla's gun and handed it to the sheriff. "Courier this over to the lab. It's probably the gun that was used in the other shootings."

"Good work," Sheriff Hardin said. "I'll drive Charla to the jail and let Dr. McGrath take care of moving McLandon's body to the morgue."

"Make sure he goes by the book. We want every piece of evidence possible to make sure Charla's arrest and confession sticks."

Hardin made a low sound in his throat. "Don't worry. I want this over with just the same as you do so peace can be restored in Comanche Creek."

One of the medics approached. "How is the deputy?" Cabe asked.

"He took a hard blow to the head, but he should be all right. We're transporting him to the hospital now."

"I'll check on him later," the sheriff said.

The medics went back to Spears and loaded him in

the ambulance, and Jessie trembled. God, the past few days had been a nightmare.

"I'm going to drive Jessie back to the house, Hardin," Cabe said. "Call me if you need anything."

Jessie tore her gaze away from Charla locked in the police car. Still, the sight of the dead body on her father's land sent a shiver through her.

Cabe took her elbow and guided her to the rental Jeep. By the time they reached her cabin and went inside, a tremble had started deep inside her that made her legs wobble.

Cabe caught her arm. "You're shaking, Jessie."

"I don't know why," she said, hating the quiver to her voice. "It's over now."

Cabe turned her to face him and stroked her arms. "You did great back there, but now the adrenaline is wearing off. It's a natural reaction." He pulled her toward the bathroom. "Come on, a hot shower will do wonders."

She nodded numbly, the sound of his strong masculine voice so hypnotic that the images of the dead man faded, and memories of what they'd been doing before the explosion returned.

She welcomed the reprieve from the horror and embraced the hunger that ripped through her. Cabe was here now. He had saved her life.

He would leave once Charla confessed to the other two murders.

She couldn't let him walk away without being with him.

"Come with me, Cabe," she whispered.

His dark brown eyes skated over her, searching. Desire flashed in the depths but also caution.

"You've had a rough night, Jessie. You need rest."

Her heart swelled at the concern in his gruff voice. "No, I need you, Cabe."

Raw need darkened his eyes, and his breath hissed out. Still, for a moment, he stood stock still, and she thought he was going to turn her down and leave.

But emotions replaced the mask of control in his eyes, and he pressed a hand to her cheek. "If anything had happened to you," he murmured gruffly, "I couldn't have stood it."

"Nothing happened," she said softly.

A muscle ticked in his jaw. "But I let Charla get to you."

She pressed a kiss to his palm. "You saved my life, Cabe."

A heartbeat of silence stretched between them, then hunger flared in his expression, and she saw him relent to the heat between them.

With a sultry smile, she led him to the shower. Muttering her name in a throaty whisper, he reached for her shirt, and slowly unfastened the buttons, then eased the garment off her shoulders.

His gaze greedily raked over her chest.

A slow smile twitched at her lips, just before he tilted his head and claimed her mouth with his. Erotic sensations pummeled her as he probed her mouth apart with his tongue and trailed his fingers over her shoulders.

There were too many clothes between them.

Heat enflamed her as their movements became more frenzied. Their clothes fell to the floor in a mad rush, but she paused to drink in his heavenly body. Big muscles that bunched in his arms and chest, a smooth, corded torso that tapered to a trim waist and thick thighs. And his sex, huge and hard, jutted toward her in invitation.

She trembled again, the chill inside her earlier turning into a minefield of hot, explosive aching.

He paused to stare at her, too, his dark gaze roving from her breasts to her hips and then her heat. A feral gleam lit his eyes, and he made a guttural sound of need that brought erotic sensations cascading across her body.

"You are so damn beautiful, Jessie." He trailed his hands over her bare shoulders, then flipped on the warm water and urged her beneath the spray. He reached for the sponge and soaked it, then traced it down her body, pausing to watch her skin bead with the soap bubbles.

She moaned as her nipples hardened, turning to turgid peaks, then he dropped the soapy sponge and used his hands to tease and explore her. She did the same, her fingers gliding over firm taut muscles, diving into his hair and pulling him close for another kiss. Tongues danced and mated, their bodies slid against one another, and he flipped off the water, grabbed a towel and hastily dried them.

"I can't wait any longer," he said in a passion-glazed voice, then scooped her into his arms.

Jessie feathered her fingers through his hair, brushing it from his forehead. "Then don't."

In three quick strides, he crossed the room and eased her onto the bed. Desperate to feel him inside her, she reached for him, clawing at his shoulders as he knelt above her and cupped her face between his hands.

She wanted the moment to last forever. To know that he wouldn't leave after they made love.

But Cabe and her long-term was impossible. Men always left. Nothing good ever lasted.

So she closed her eyes and savored the moment.

CABE'S HEART POUNDED as he rose above Jessie. She was so damn beautiful and wonderful that he felt humbled that she wanted him.

Her red hair fanned across the pillow, and her rosy lips were parted in invitation. He drank in the image of her opening to him, of her nipples pink-tipped and pebbled, waiting for his mouth. Her sweet feminine scent sent shards of need through him. And her slick heat lay at the center of her creamy thighs, a home waiting for him.

Hungry to taste her, he kissed her lips first, deeply, plunging his tongue inside her mouth in a teasing dance. His breath caught at the sound of her excited moan, and he dragged his lips down to her throat, gliding his tongue along the sensitive skin of her earlobe, then paving a delicious path to her breasts.

One hand twisted her left nipple between his fingers while his lips sucked her other one into his mouth. She bucked, rubbing her foot along his calf, her body quivering as he suckled her. He laved both breasts, his hunger mounting at the feel of her soft skin brushing his, her hips undulating beneath him.

She threaded her fingers into his hair, then clutched his shoulders, urging him to enter her. But he wanted to prolong her pleasure, so he dove south toward the heart of her femininity, licking her belly, then he parted her legs and swept his tongue over the sensitive flesh of her inner thighs.

"Cabe…"

A smile curved his mouth at her breathy sound, and he licked his way toward her heat, then over her swollen nub, teasing her until her body began to convulse with her orgasm. The taste of her honeyed release sent erotic sensations assaulting him.

He had to have her.

Groaning her name, he rose above her again, then guided his erection toward her damp chamber. She lifted her hips, her body trembling, begging for him to fill her.

Enflamed by her hunger, he reached for his pants on the floor, grabbed a condom, ripped it open and sheathed himself.

She was fumbling to help him, stroking his shaft, urging him to hurry. Heaving a breath to control himself before he burst, he kissed her again, then thrust inside her.

She was so small, tight, her insides clenching as he pounded inside her. Panting, she wrapped her legs around his waist, allowing him even deeper access. Excited by her throaty moans, he stroked her over and over, cupping her hips in his hands and building a frantic rhythm until her body quivered, and she climaxed again. Her cries of pleasure triggered his own release, and his own orgasm built, powerful and intense.

His chest clenched and spasms rocked his body. He'd made love to a lot of women, but never had he felt so connected, as if he'd lost his heart and soul in the moment.

The thought sent a lightninglike bolt of fear through him. No, he couldn't fall for Jessie. Couldn't allow himself to feel anything but the pleasure of the moment.

They belonged to two different worlds. She was a Becker. And he was a Texas Ranger, not a man with a woman in his future.

Chapter Twelve

Jessie curled into Cabe's arms, her body still humming from the aftermath of their lovemaking.

Lord help her, but she didn't want him to ever leave. She wanted to have him in her bed every night, holding her, making love to her, groaning her name as he came inside her.

The fear that she'd fallen in love with the Ranger gnawed at her, threatening to ruin the moment, but she pushed it away.

Nothing mattered now except that she was safe, that Cabe was holding her, that they'd finally found the killer tormenting Comanche Creek.

Content with his big body beside her, she fell into a deep sleep. Dreams of Cabe filled the night.

The two of them were riding across the pasture on horseback with the wind whipping through her hair. His Stetson was cocked to the side, giving her a glimpse of the sexy smile that he saved only for her. The grass was green, wildflowers dotted the hill, and the air smelled of honeysuckle and spring.

They galloped over to the pond, then climbed down, and Cabe suddenly knelt in front of her and took her hand. Tears pooled in her eyes as he removed a velvet ring box from his pocket and opened it. A stunning engagement ring glittered up at her.

"Oh, my God, that's beautiful."

Moonlight highlighted his bronzed skin, and he suddenly looked nervous. "Will you marry me, Jessie?"

Pure joy flooded her chest. "Yes, of course, I will. I love you, Cabe."

His hand shook as he slid the ring on her hand, then swept her into his arms and kissed her. "I love you, too."

Suddenly the shrill ringing of her cell phone jarred her from the blissful dream. Jessie sat up, searching the bed for Cabe, but he stood at the window, his back to her.

"Cabe."

He slowly turned toward her, and her heart clenched at the turmoil in his eyes. He'd tugged on his jeans, but hadn't buttoned the top button and they hung low on his hips, making him look sinfully sexy. Her gaze was drawn to his bare chest, then the bulge in his fly, and she ached to beg him to come back to bed.

But her phone trilled again, and the hunger in his eyes faded as his look turned brooding and dark.

"Your phone is ringing." His hooded gaze raked over her breasts where the sheet had fallen down, and her body tingled. She wanted him, needed him. But he didn't make a move to come back to her.

Feeling vulnerable, she jerked up the sheet, then scrambled to reach her phone on the nightstand. "Hello."

"It's Lolita, Miss Jessie. Your father…he had a rough night. I think you should come. I've called the doctor."

Worry immediately knotted her shoulders. "I'll be right there."

Cabe's eyes narrowed. "What's wrong?"

"My father had a bad night," Jessie said, reaching for her shirt. "I…want to talk, Cabe, but—"

"You have to go," he said matter-of-factly. "And so do I."

She tugged on her shirt and pulled it together, then walked over to him. The remnants of her dream taunted her. "Cabe, about last night—"

He pressed a finger to her lips. "We both know I'm leaving Comanche Creek, Jessie." He gestured outside. "This ranch is your home. I don't belong here."

Hurt knifed through Jessie. The scent of his skin, of their sex, clung to him, making her belly clench. She finally understood how her mother could become so enamored with a man that she'd throw herself at him. The thought of never seeing Cabe again terrified her even more than the thought of getting hurt.

Had she become like her father over the years, closing herself off to relationships because she couldn't face rejection?

Maybe it was time she stopped allowing fear to rule her life.

Inhaling a deep breath for courage, she decided to be honest with herself and with him. "I…love you, Cabe. We could make it work if you wanted."

He shut his eyes for a moment, but his posture stiffened, and he clenched his jaw.

When he finally looked at her again, regret shone in his eyes. "I'm sorry, Jessie. You want this ranch, a family, Comanche Creek as a home. Things I can't give you."

Pain rocked through her. She'd given him her heart, yet he didn't love her.

"Now, go to your father. I need to interrogate Charla, and tie up the loose ends to the investigation."

Without another word, he grabbed his shirt, his gun and jacket, then pulled on his boots, and walked out the door.

Jessie waited, hoped, prayed he'd look back, but he didn't.

WALKING OUT OF JESSIE'S bedroom was one of the hardest things Cabe had ever done.

Last night had been so damn…erotic.

Emotions he'd never thought he'd feel had crowded his chest while he'd watched Jessie sleep. Curled in his arms, she looked like an angel. He'd felt himself sinking into fantasies, falling for her, *needing* her.

He didn't want to need anyone.

Yet, for a brief moment he'd imagined sleeping with her every night. Making love to her every day.

Sharing a life with her that would last forever…

But that was impossible. Their two worlds divided them.

Loving someone meant risking losing them just as he'd lost his mother and brother years ago.

He never wanted to endure that kind of pain again.

Still, part of him wanted to go with her to see her

father, wanted to help shoulder the burden of his illness and any other problem she encountered.

Dammit. He had to go. Finish tying up the case.

Jessie was tough and strong and would survive just fine without him.

I love you, Cabe…

No, she didn't love him. She couldn't. She'd just been through a terrifying ordeal, and he had been close by to comfort her. She would forget him after he left, find another man to hold her, comfort her, make love to her.

Anger shot through him at the thought, protective and possessive instincts surfacing.

Dammit. He had to let her go.

Daylight shimmered off the drive as he slid into the Jeep, jammed the key into the ignition and peeled from the drive. He forced thoughts of Jessie from his mind as he left the ranch and drove to the jail.

Sheriff Hardin was already in his office, and gestured to the coffeepot so Cabe helped himself to a cup. "Have you been here all night?" Cabe asked.

Hardin shook his head. "No, I left one of the deputies here to guard Charla."

"Did you get Charla's official statement?"

"No, she was so hysterical I had to call the shrink who worked with her at the pysch ward when she was admitted before. He came over and gave her a sleeping pill to calm her."

"You think she'll try to plea out on an insanity charge?"

Hardin shrugged. "Either way, we have to make sure she stays locked up. She might have killed the first victim out of panic, but the others were premeditated. And using that clay to glue the victims' eyes shut to imitate a ritualistic burial, that was damn near cunning."

"I agree. Call her doctor back and tell them we need a blood sample to confirm that it was her blood in the paint used on the victims' faces."

Hardin nodded. "I'll take care of it."

Cabe adjusted his Stetson. "I'd like to question her again. I want her confession in writing."

Hardin glanced outside. "Jerry Collier is on his way. He's representing Charla."

Cabe shook his head. He still didn't like the sleazy lawyer. He could have his own agenda—he probably wanted to make sure Charla didn't implicate him in the phony land deal.

Hardin strode down the hall to escort Charla to the interrogation room. Just as he'd said, Collier arrived, clutching a briefcase in his hand, a pompous look on his face.

"Ranger Navarro, have you questioned my client without me?"

Cabe silently cursed. "Isn't this a conflict of interest for you, Collier?"

"Absolutely not. Now take me to Charla."

Cabe retrieved the tape recorder from his crime kit along with the case folder, and he and Collier met Hardin and Charla in the interrogation room.

The normally flamboyant woman looked disheveled and withered as she sank into the straight, hard chair. Her face was pale, makeup smudged, and purple bruises darkened the skin beneath her bloodshot eyes.

Cabe pulled out a chair and faced her. "Charla, let's start from the beginning."

She stared up at him with glassy eyes. "I told you everything last night."

Cabe removed a picture of Lattimer and Phillips, pointing out the way their eyes were glued shut. "You lured these men out to the Becker land and killed them, then used clay from Jonah Becker's land to make the ochre to glue their eyes shut."

Her mouth tightened as she studied the grotesque photos of the men. "Yes, I told you I did. They wanted to expose me and the deal I made with Jonah."

"Did Jonah know the land belonged to the Native Americans?" Cabe asked.

She ran a trembling hand through her hair, and sighed wearily. Her normally manicured fingernails were jagged and chipped from where she'd chewed on them during the night.

"No. Jonah hasn't been well," Charla said in a tired voice. "Billy and I doctored the paperwork to make it look as if the land originally belonged to Jonah's great-great-grandfather."

Cabe nodded. "And Marcie knew all this, so you killed her?"

Charla jerked her head up, shaking her head wildly. "I told you I didn't kill Marcie or Daniel Taabe. And I certainly didn't kill my husband."

Cabe and Hardin exchanged frustrated looks. Why would she deny killing them when she already had four murders on her head?

"But you killed McLandon?" Cabe pressed.

"Yes," she cried. "Yes, I did because he was going to ruin me forever."

"That's enough," Collier interjected. "My client has a diminished mental capacity."

Hardin glared at Collier. "Your client is ruthless, and confessed to premeditated murder."

"You mean McLandon was going to expose you, don't you, Charla?" Cabe snarled.

Charla broke down and began to sob again, muttering incoherently.

Cabe and Hardin spent twenty more minutes reviewing the case details, but she still refused to admit that she'd killed Marcie, Daniel or Billy.

Cabe's cell phone vibrated and he checked the number. Wyatt.

"Excuse me. I need to take this." He gestured to the sheriff. "Get Charla's confession typed up and make sure she signs it."

Hardin agreed, and Cabe stepped from the room. "Sergeant Navarro."

"Cabe, it's Wyatt. The Captain is satisfied that you've solved this case and is ready to disband the task force. He's already spoken to the press and announced that Charla Whitley was responsible for all the murders and is in custody."

Cabe cursed. Charla's confession—or lack of one regarding Marcie's, Billy's and Daniel's deaths—troubled him. "We can't do that just yet. Hardin and I just interrogated Charla again, and she insists she didn't kill Marcie, Daniel or Billy."

Wyatt made a frustrated sound. "Hell. Then keep

pushing, Cabe. I'll stall for time, but I want every detail to fit before you pull out."

Cabe agreed, then snapped his phone shut. If Charla hadn't killed Marcie, Billy and Daniel, then their killer was still at large.

His stomach knotted.

And Jessie might still be in danger.

"DADDY, PLEASE CALM DOWN," Jessie cried. "I hate to see you so agitated."

Her father had been pacing the study, pulling at his hair, and making a ticking sound with his teeth. "It's the ghosts, those damn Indian spirits," he ranted. "They're haunting me, Jessie. They beat their war drums all night long. They're coming for me."

Jessie twisted her hands together. Cabe claimed he felt and heard the spirits on the land, but now her father heard them, too? Was it possible? Or was her dad hallucinating?

"Daddy, Dr. Pickford is on his way." She reached for her father to urge him into a chair, but he shoved her hands away and continued pacing.

"I don't need a doctor. I need someone to get rid of these damn ghosts. Give them back the land if that'll satisfy them."

A knock sounded at the door, and Lolita poked her head in. "Dr. Pickford's here."

Jessie sighed, feeling helpless. Her father needed medical treatment, maybe even hospitalization. "Thanks, Lolita. Please send him in."

Her father swirled around, walked to his cabinet, removed a bottle of Scotch and poured himself a glass.

"I know you think I'm crazy, Jessie, but I'm not. There's something awful going on here at the ranch. I wish to hell I'd never bought that land."

"So do I, Daddy," Jessie said as the doctor entered the room. That sale had caused so many deaths so far. Maybe he was right. Maybe the land was cursed.

"Just let Dr. Pickford take care of you, Dad."

He grabbed her hands in a death-grip. "And you take care of the ranch, Jessie. Promise me you'll do that, and that you'll get rid of that Ranger."

Except she didn't want Cabe to leave Comanche Creek. "Dad, Ranger Navarro will be gone soon. He arrested Charla Whitley last night for those murders, so hopefully soon things will settle down."

Her phone buzzed in her purse, and she gave her father a quick kiss on the cheek. "I'll be back in a little while." She spoke to the doctor, then left the room, dug her phone from her purse, and flipped it open. "Hello."

"Jessie, listen to me. Charla Whitley didn't kill Marcie. I know it."

The woman's voice sounded strained. Frightened. Familiar. "Who is this?"

"Linda Lantz." Her breathing rattled between them as if she might be running. "Oh, God, Jessie. I know I should have come forward, but I was afraid I'd end up dead like the others."

Jessie's lungs constricted. "Linda? I was afraid you were dead. Where are you?"

Linda started to cry. "I'm scared, Jessie."

"I know," Jessie said softly. "But the Rangers will protect you. Cabe Navarro is here. You can trust him."

Linda sighed shakily. "All right, I'm at the Bluebon-net Inn under the name of Megan Burgess."

"I'll be right there." Jessie snapped her phone closed.

Dear God, Linda knew who had killed Marcie. And the killer was after her.

She had to hurry.

Chapter Thirteen

An uneasy feeling stabbed at Cabe as he and the sheriff retreated to Hardin's office.

"Charla signed the confession," Hardin said. "But Collier will try to convince the judge to commit her to a mental institution instead of serving time in prison."

"You think the judge will agree?" Cabe asked.

Hardin shrugged. "I don't know. But as long as she can't hurt anyone else, I don't see as it matters. And with her confession about the illegal land deal, the land can be returned to the Comanche Nation so you can soothe those ruffled feathers."

"True." Although Jonah and Trace Becker wouldn't be pleased.

Cabe leaned against the doorjamb. "Lieutneant Colter called, and the Ranger Captain wanted to pull us from the case."

"So you'll be leaving town?" Hardin asked.

Cabe huffed. "Not yet. It still bothers me that Charla insists she didn't kill Marcie, Billy and Daniel."

Hardin scrubbed his hand through his hair. "Yeah,

that doesn't make sense. She's already confessed to multiple murders. What's two or three more?"

Cabe grabbed a chair and parked himself in it. "Maybe we should review our suspect list."

Hardin nodded. "First, Deputy Shane Tolbert, who was found holding the Ruger that murdered Marcie. Then Jerry Collier, who handled the land deal and works for Becker. Then Jonah Becker."

"We can rule out Jonah."

Hardin slanted him a sideways grin. "Why? Because you have the hots for Jessie?"

Cabe gritted his teeth. "No. Because he's ill and having memory problems. That's the reason Jessie has been handling things in town and with the task force. They didn't want anyone to know he was sick."

"You're sure this illness is for real?"

"Yeah. I saw him myself. He's not strong enough physically or mentally to have pulled off those murders. In his confused state, he could easily have been duped into the land deal." Cabe paused. "Of course, Trace is still on the list. He's conniving, spoiled and jealous of Jessie."

"What about Ellie?"

"The hair fibers I found at the original cadaver site didn't belong to her. But she and Trace are having an affair, so I suppose they could have conspired. Although I can't imagine Ellie allowing any artifacts to be removed from the land. And if she'd known it was a sacred burial ground, she would have moved hell or high water to keep the property in the custody of the Comanches."

"Maybe Trace lied to Ellie."

Cabe nodded, following his train of thought. "And he wanted to protect his daddy's investment."

"He could have killed Daniel because Daniel was onto the truth. And if Trace is in love with Ellie, getting Daniel out of the way paved the road for Ellie to move up the political chain."

"Ellie does have high political aspirations," Cabe admitted. The uneasy feeling he'd had earlier escalated. "I'm going to phone Jessie and warn her to stay put, that another killer may still be at large. Then let's plan some kind of trap to draw the second killer out of hiding."

He punched in Jessie's number, but the phone rang and rang and no one answered. Finally the voice mail kicked on.

"Jessie, this is Cabe. A killer still may be out there, so stay with your father." He snapped his phone shut. He didn't like the fact that she hadn't answered.

He never should have left her at her house. What if the killer had already gotten to her?

JESSIE'S CELL PHONE BUZZED in her purse as she parked on Main Street, but it rolled over to voice mail before she could dig it out. She cut the engine, then checked the message box in case Linda had changed her mind. But the message was from Cabe.

He had called to warn her that another killer was still at large. She started to return his call, but Linda had sounded spooked, and Jessie was afraid that she'd run again if she didn't hurry to her.

Throwing the car door open, she slung her purse over

her shoulder, checking around her for strangers as she walked up to the porch to the Bluebonnet Inn. Praying Linda hadn't already bolted, she opened the front door. The owner, Betty Alice, was carrying a tray of tea and shortbread to the buffet in the dining room.

"Why, Jessie Becker, what are you doing here?" Betty Alice said with a grin.

"I came to meet one of your guests, Betty."

The plump woman's eyebrows shot up. "Really? A young man?"

Jessie's cheeks stained pink as she remembered her lovemaking with Cabe. She wished she was here to meet him for another romantic rendezvous.

"No, Betty. A woman named Megan Burgess."

"Oh, yes, that sweet girl. She's in the pink room. Do you want me to ring her and tell her you're here?"

"No, thanks. I'll just go straight to the room. She's expecting me."

Betty Alice threw her fingers up in a wave, and Jessie rushed up the staircase, then down the hall to the pink room, the room where Betty housed most of her female guests. It was decorated with antique furniture and a balcony opened to the second-floor porch.

The door was closed, so Jessie knocked. "Linda... Megan?"

Her pulse raced as she waited, and she thought she heard movement inside, so she knocked again. When Linda didn't answer, she jiggled the doorknob and the door swung open. She made a quick scan of the room and bath, but they were empty.

The door to the porch was open, so she crossed the

room and stepped onto the porch, hoping to find Linda outside. But the porch was empty, too.

Frantic, she glanced down at the gardens, and saw a few people on the sidewalk on Main Street, but no Linda. A movement caught her eyes, and she noted a tall woman with black hair wearing a scarf weaving through the crowd. She'd seen the same woman at the town meeting.

Linda had been blonde, but she was using a fake name. What if she'd dyed her hair?

Something must have spooked her, but what? Had the killer found her?

Deciding she'd walk to the jail from the inn, meet Cabe and explain about Linda's call, she left the room, hurried down the stairs and rushed out the front door.

But just as she stepped from the porch, Deputy Shane Tolbert appeared. "Jessie?"

"Yes?"

"I was just at the jail. That Ranger asked me to escort you home."

Anger slammed into Jessie. Was Cabe going to avoid her now they'd made love? Pawn her off on another cop? And Shane Tolbert? She didn't even like the man. "Why didn't he come himself?"

Deputy Tolbert shrugged. "I don't know. I'm just following orders." He gestured toward his squad car, which was parked behind her Jeep. "Get in and I'll drive you."

"I can drive myself," Jessie said emphatically. "Besides I want to go to the jail and talk to Cabe. I have some information about the killer."

Shane's brow shot up. "Tell me and I'll pass it on."

So Cabe was avoiding her. "I spoke with a woman who claims she knows who killed Marcie and Daniel Taabe. I was supposed to meet her here, but when I went to her room, she'd disappeared."

"I see." His eyes turned cold, his voice hard. "Get in the car, Jessie."

He reached for her arm, but she jerked away. She refused to let Cabe dismiss her. "No. I told you I'm going to the jail."

Shane grabbed her arm again so tightly this time she winced. Then he pulled his gun from his holster and pointed it at her waist. "I said get in the car."

Fear rolled through Jessie as he shoved her into the backseat of his car, forced her to lie down, then slammed the butt of the gun against her head. Pain ricocheted through her temple, and the world spun as he jumped in the driver's seat and raced off.

Dear God, he had killed Marcie and Daniel.

And now he was going to kill her, too.

CABE HAD TO FIND JESSIE. While Sheriff Hardin phoned Livvy to check on her, Cabe called Jessie's house, desperate to hear her voice, and hating that he was desperate. But if anything had happened to her...

"Becker residence. Lolita speaking."

"This is Ranger Navarro. Is Jessie there?"

"No, sir," Lolita said. "She left a while back."

"Do you know where she was going?"

"No, she didn't say." The woman's voice dropped a decibel. "Why, Ranger Navarro? Is something wrong? Has something happened to Miss Jessie?"

Cabe gritted his teeth. "Not that I know of. I'm just trying to reach her. If she phones you or comes back to the house, please have her call me."

Cabe thanked her, hung up, then phoned her brother. "Trace, this is Ranger Navarro. Where are you?"

"Why do you want to know? So you can harass me again?"

"I'm looking for your sister, Trace. Is she with you?"

"Hell, no. I thought you were glued to her."

Cabe silently cursed. Trace could be lying. "I asked you where you are."

"I'd rather not say."

"Listen to me, Trace, if you have your sister or have hurt her, you'll answer to me."

"I told you my sister isn't with me," Trace bellowed. "I'm in Austin. I came over here to talk to one of my father's doctors about more tests."

Cabe clenched the phone. Dammit. Trace's heated response had the ring of truth to it. "If you hear from her, tell her to call me."

Snapping his phone shut, he headed out the door of the jail. Maybe Jessie had ridden back to the burial sites on her property. But a young woman with shoulder-length black hair barreled into him. He threw up his hands and caught her by the shoulders.

"Help, you have to help me!" she cried.

"Whoa." Cabe pulled her into the front office and shut the door. "Calm down and tell me what's going on."

"My name is Megan Burgess…" She paused to take a breath. She was trembling, her green eyes flashing with fear. "I mean Linda Lantz."

"Linda Lantz? You worked for Jessie and disappeared two years ago?"

She bobbed her head up and down, then pressed her hand to her chest to catch her breath. "Yes, but I left town because I was afraid someone would try to kill me."

He noticed her black hair, remembered the photo he'd seen of the blonde Jessie had identified as Linda Lantz, and realized that the two dyed strands he'd found at the burial site belonged to her.

"Come on and sit down," he said, coaxing her to a chair. "Tell me everything."

She twisted her hands in her lap. "I was working on the Becker ranch two years ago when I saw Marcie fake her kidnapping and death. But then I noticed a man in the shadows and he saw me, so I ran." She lifted a hand to her cheek. "I left town, had plastic surgery and dyed my hair so he couldn't find me."

Cabe's chest tightened. "Did you recognize the man?"

She shivered. "Yes."

"But you didn't come forward?" Cabe asked angrily.

"No," she whispered raggedly. "I told you I was scared. But then when I heard about those bodies being found, and that Marcie was really murdered, I came back to town. I knew I had to do something, but I didn't know whom to trust. Then I saw you were with Jessie, and I was afraid you'd blame me, that you would arrest me for not coming forward sooner. I thought…I hoped you'd find out the truth before anyone else got hurt."

Cabe gripped her arms. "Linda, who killed Marcie?"

Her lower lip quivered, and she sucked air through her teeth. "Deputy Tolbert."

Cabe's heart pounded.

"I called Jessie to tell her," she rushed on, "and she came to meet me at the Bluebonnet Inn. But then he showed up."

"Deputy Tolbert showed up?"

She nodded miserably.

Cabe's blood ran cold. "Then what happened?"

Panic and fear strained her features as a sob escaped her. "He took Jessie."

Chapter Fourteen

Cabe's heart lurched to his throat. The mere idea that Jessie's life hung in the hands of a ruthless killer made him furious.

"Listen to me, Linda, where was Deputy Tolbert taking Jessie?"

"I don't know," Linda whispered. "I really don't know. He just shoved her in the back of his car and hit her with the butt of his gun."

Cabe sucked in a sharp breath. "Was she all right?"

"I don't know." She swiped at more tears. "He must have knocked her unconscious, because she didn't get up. Then he jumped in the front seat and sped off."

Cabe stood. He had to take action. Every second that passed meant Tolbert was getting farther and father away with Jessie.

JESSIE SLOWLY ROUSED back to consciousness, but her head throbbed and nausea clogged her throat. She wiggled, determined to escape, but her hands were tied behind her back, and she was gagged.

The police car hit a bump, and pain ricocheted through her skull as the car rumbled across a road that had to be dirt and gravel. How long had he been driving? How far were they from Comanche Creek?

How would Cabe ever find her?

Despair clawed at her chest, and tears pooled in her eyes. Cabe had no idea Shane had killed Marcie, much less kidnapped her. He didn't even know Linda was still alive.

Had Shane killed her, too? If so, where was her body?

Feeling panicky, the urge to sit up and scream at him, to beg and plead with him to let her go, drummed through her. Yet what good would that do?

She blinked back tears, frantically struggling for control. She had to stay calm, try to talk to Shane, stall.

Wait for an opportune moment so she could escape.

The past few years of her life flashed back in vivid clarity. Her college years where she'd held herself back from relationships. Her pride in earning her degree.

The fights with her mother.

Her vow to be different, not to be led around by a man, or to lose her heart. But it was too late for that.

She had lost her heart to Cabe.

But he had rebuked her. Didn't love her.

Her chest clenched as her dreams died. Secretly she had wanted stability. Her mother's love. Her father's. The family that had been broken years ago.

And she wanted it with Cabe.

But that would never happen.

Still, she would survive. She had to.

Her father needed her.

The car swerved, then spun right, the terrain growing even more rocky and uneven. Gravel crunched beneath the tires, and she focused on the sounds outside, hoping for a clue as to where Shane was taking her.

The river…she heard the river raging over rocks. It had to be the Colorado River, which wasn't too far from Comanche Creek. Shane slowed slightly, and her heart raced as she glanced up at the hulking trees and realized the place was secluded.

Suddenly the car bounced over another rut, gravel spewed, and he screeched to a stop. The movement jarred her, and she almost rolled off the seat and onto the floor, but caught herself with her foot.

Shane climbed out, then jerked the back door open, and grabbed her arm. She tried to remain limp, pretended to be unconscious, but he shook her as he dragged her from the car.

"Come on, Jessie, you should be awake by now."

His icy, harsh voice sent a shiver up her spine, and she opened her eyes and gave him a hate-filled look.

With a vicious yank, he dragged her across the rocky terrain. "You know too much now."

Jessie gulped back fear, visually assessing her surroundings. They were in a secluded spot by the river, and an old log cabin sat near the bank, shrouded by bushes and trees. The place looked run-down, and weeds choked the front porch as if no one had been here in years.

The isolation of it made her tremble in blinding panic. Even if Linda had survived and mustered up enough courage to go to the police, Cabe would never know to look for her out here.

She tried to speak to him, but the gag caught the sound. Shane cursed, then pulled it from her mouth and threw her up against a tree.

"Where are we?" Jessie asked in a ragged whisper. The rough bark bit into her back and arms, the vile stench of a dead animal wafted around them.

"My father's cabin," Shane growled. "But don't get your hopes up. No one knows this place even exists."

"Your father does," Jessie cried. "Do you think he'd want you to do this? To kill me?"

"My father loved me. He'll do anything to protect me."

"That's right, Ben is in jail now, isn't he?" Jessie snarled. "All because you're a murderer."

Shane raised his hand and slapped her hard across the cheek. Perspiration trickled down Jessie's back, the sting of the blow making her ears ring. "You're good at beating women, aren't you, Shane?"

"Shut up, Jessie. You should have stayed out of this." Shane pressed the gun to her temple. "Now tell me where Linda is."

Hope budded in Jessie's chest. If Shane wanted to know Linda's whereabouts, she must still be alive. Determined not to reveal how terrified she really was, Jessie jutted up her chin. "I don't know."

"She called you?"

"Yes," Jessie said. "She told me what you'd done, that you killed Marcie." Jessie sucked in a sharp breath. "Why, Shane? Because she broke up with you?"

"She loved me," Shane said in a sharp tone. "She loved me and we should have been together."

"But she discovered that you're a brute," Jessie said.

"That's why she left you. But you couldn't stand that, could you? You were a bully, and she was so scared of you that she faked her own kidnapping and death."

His hand connected with her face again, this time even harder. Despite her bravado, tears stung her eyes and escaped. She clenched her jaw to keep from screaming.

Shane pressed the gun to her temple. "Tell me, Jessie. If you don't, I'm going to kill you."

"You don't have to do that," Jessie whispered.

A leering, evil look flickered in his eyes, a maddening look that made her heart thunder.

"I have nothing left to lose, Jessie," Shane bit out. "So either tell me where to find her, or you're a dead woman."

CABE CALLED HARDIN IN TO the front office, introduced him to Linda, and explained what had happened.

"You saw Marcie fake her kidnapping and death?" Sheriff Hardin asked.

Linda nodded miserably. "But Shane came after me and I ran. I was…so scared." She swiped at tears rolling down her cheeks. "Maybe if I'd come forward then, these other murders wouldn't have happened."

Cabe almost felt sorry for her. *Almost.*

But Jessie was in the hands of a madman now, a dangerous cold-blooded killer.

Hardin propped his hip on the edge of the desk. "Hell, Livvy's going to have a fit. She was the one who figured out that Shane's prints had been planted on that gun."

"It's not her fault. Shane intentionally cleaned the gun, then planted just enough prints to confuse us and force you to release him," Cabe said in disgust.

Hardin pulled at his chin. "I hope she sees it that way." He turned to Linda. "Did you see Shane kill Marcie?"

A pained look crossed her face. "Yes. After she disappeared the first time, we connected. We came back here to make things right, but Shane found Marcie in the cabin. I ran outside and hid in the woods, but then he shot her."

Cabe scrubbed his hand over the back of his neck. "We have to find Shane before he hurts Jessie." He turned to the sheriff. "You know Shane better than anyone, Hardin. Do you have any idea where he'd take Jessie?"

"To his place maybe?"

"I doubt he'd be foolish enough to do that, but why don't you check?" Cabe suggested. "I'll call Lieutenant Colter and brief him, then question Shane's father and see if he might know."

"I'll put out an APB for Shane on my way to Tolbert's place and alert the county deputies to watch out for his car."

"Check out Ben's place as well as Charla's," Cabe said. "He might hide out in one of those."

"Right." Hardin gestured to Linda. "Come on, Linda. I'll drop you with Ranger Hutton, so I can make sure you're safe."

Cabe punched in Wyatt's number and gave him a quick update.

"Son of a bitch," Wyatt muttered. "I never did trust Tolbert."

"We have to find him fast," Cabe said. "He's already killed. He won't hesitate to take another life."

"I'll see what I can dig up on him. Maybe he owns some other property where he might take Jessie."

A place where Shane might dump her body. The

unspoken words hung between them, making Cabe's pulse pound.

"Let me know if you find anything," Cabe said, already heading to the back of the building toward Tolbert's cell. "Ben's still here. I'll see what he knows."

"I doubt he'll cooperate," Wyatt said. "He's protected Shane at every turn."

"He'll talk," Cabe said through clenched teeth.

Wyatt started to say something, but Cabe cut him off and disconnected the call. He didn't give a damn right now about protocol or Tolbert's rights or his job.

Jessie's life was all that mattered.

He grabbed the keys to the jail cells, praying it wasn't already too late.

Rolling his hands into fists, he stalked down the row of cells. Charla was hunched on the cot, her eyes glazed as she stared at her hands. She looked pitiful, dazed, in shock, as if she'd slipped into a catatonic state.

She and Shane were friends. If Ben didn't cough up something useful, he'd question Charla.

Ben sat up from his cot when Cabe approached, his face haggard, his hair disheveled, his eyes filled with anger.

Cabe unlocked the cell and stepped inside. "I need to talk to you, Tolbert."

"What the hell do you want?"

"We have a witness who says that Shane killed Marcie. Now your son has kidnapped Jessie Becker at gunpoint."

Ben lowered his head into his hands and muttered a curse. "Dear God…"

"You'd better be praying," Cabe said sharply. "And

you'd better be talking. Because if Shane kills Jessie, I'm holding you responsible, too."

"I don't care about myself," Ben muttered. "All I care about is my son."

"What about Jessie Becker?" Cabe growled. "She's an innocent woman, Ben. How can you not help us?"

"I can't believe this is happening," Ben said in a brittle tone. "He won't hurt Jessie. He won't."

Cabe jerked him by the collar. "He killed Marcie, and maybe Daniel and Billy. What's one more death to him?"

Ben snapped his head up, his expression pained. "No…Shane is not a killer."

"Shane *is* a murderer. And if he kills Jessie, I'll make sure he receives the death sentence."

"No, you can't do that," Ben hissed.

"I can and I will," Cabe ground out. "Murder during a kidnapping is a capital offense. And Texas has the highest rate of executions in the nation."

"You son of a bitch—"

"Where would Shane take Jessie, Ben?"

Ben's eyes bulged with fear. "I don't know."

"Come on, Ben." Cabe tightened his grip on the man's collar, choking Ben. "Do either of you own a cabin or property other than your houses in Comanche Creek?"

Ben's weathered face reddened as he struggled to breathe. "I can't let you hurt my son."

"But you'll let him kill an innocent woman and go to death row," Cabe said. "What kind of man are you?"

Cabe's cell phone trilled, and he reluctantly released Ben, and checked the caller ID. Lieutenant Colter.

He punched the connect button, one eye trained on Ben in case he tried to escape. "Navarro."

"Cabe, Ben owns an old fishing cabin on the Colorado River. It's about a half-hour drive from Comanche Creek."

Cabe gritted his teeth. A half an hour? It might as well be days away.

"I would send a chopper to see if his car is there," Wyatt continued, "but it's too remote and there's no place for it to land."

"I'm on my way." Cabe jotted down the GPS coordinates, then turned to Tolbert. "I know about your cabin," he said in a lethally calm tone. "And if I'm too late, then you and your son are going to pay."

He slammed the jail cell door shut, and jogged outside. He had to hurry.

Jessie's life hung in the balance.

Chapter Fifteen

"Shane, please don't do this," Jessie cried. "You need help."

"What I need is to know where Linda is." He jammed the gun at her back and shoved her toward the porch. She stumbled over loose rock, and nearly tripped as she climbed the steps, but he caught her arm with clawlike fingers, yanked open the screened door, and pushed her inside.

Muttering a curse, he threw her down on the floor. Jessie's knees slammed into the wood floor, pain rocketing through her bones as she struggled to catch herself. But with her hands tied behind her, it was impossible, and her shoulder slammed into the corner of the rickety pine coffee table.

She frantically glanced around the cabin for an escape route, a weapon, anything to use to defend herself. But the room was bare except for the worn plaid sofa, the stuffed trout on the wall, the photos of Shane and his father when he was younger on a fishing trip.

"Think about your dad, Shane," Jessie pleaded. "Would he want you to do this?"

Anguish darkened Shane's eyes. "My father is in jail because he was trying to protect me from going to prison. Getting arrested would kill him now."

"You think he wants you to murder again?"

"I think he wants me to stay free, and that's what I'm going to do." He grabbed her arm and yanked her up, then shoved her into one of the kitchen chairs. She stiffened as he retrieved a piece of rope dangling from his pocket, and began to tie her to the chair.

She kicked at him, but he slapped her across the face again, and she tasted blood.

"This is what we're going to do," Shane said with a mad look in his eyes. "You're going to tell me how to contact Linda, then she'll come here and we'll all have a big party."

"I don't know how to contact her," Jessie said. "She called me."

He ran to the car, then returned a minute later with her cell phone, and Jessie gritted her teeth as he scrolled through her phone log.

"Dammit, I thought you said she called you."

"She did," Jessie said. "But I don't know where she was when she called."

Shane paced, waving his gun and scraping his hand through his hair, obviously desperate.

Jessie's phone buzzed, and her stomach clenched. What if it was Linda or Cabe calling?

Shane grabbed the phone and glanced at the caller ID. A menacing smile curved his mouth as he punched the connect button.

"Hello, Ranger Navarro."

Jessie's heart raced.

"Yes, Jessie is here with me. Why don't you join us?"

Cold fear slid along Jessie's spine. If Cabe showed up, he'd kill them all.

She loved Cabe too much to let him die.

"And if you want to see Jessie alive," Shane said in a sinister tone, "then bring Linda with you."

"No," Jessie cried. "It's a trap, Cabe. Stay away!"

Shane slammed her phone shut, then stalked over and whacked the gun against her temple. The impact sent her head flying backward, and stars danced in front of her eyes.

She tried to fight it, but once again the darkness swallowed her.

CABE CURSED A BLUE streak at Tolbert's demands.

He had no intention of going back for Linda. He'd been in law enforcement long enough to know that Shane was out of control, desperate, and that he wouldn't let Jessie, Linda or him go.

Not alive.

Better he protect Linda and save Jessie.

If he had to kill Shane to do it—hell, he would have no qualms. The man deserved to die.

The Jeep ate the miles to the cabin, the sun fading and night creeping on the rugged terrain. Limestone bluffs and scrub brush dotted the horizon, the more populated area disintegrating into isolated dirt roads and cabins scattered occasionally along the Colorado River. He checked the coordinates and turned onto a side road that had never been paved, sweat beading on his forehead as the Jeep bounced over the ruts and ridges.

The quiet normally would seem peaceful, but tonight it only served to remind him that Jessie was out here alone in the hands of a killer with no way to call for help.

And no one to hear her if she did.

Before he left the vehicle, he called Hardin in for backup and gave him the coordinates. But he couldn't wait. Every minute that passed gave Tolbert time to kill Jessie.

Needing the element of surprise on his side, he crept down the dirt road, weaving around the curves and through the tangled trees, slowing a half of a mile from the place where the cabin should be. He pulled to the side of the one-way stretch, cut the engine, then slipped from the Jeep, making sure he eased the car door closed so as not to make a sound.

Images of Jessie tormented him as he slowly crept along the edge of the woods toward the cabin. Jessie riding up to him on that horse wearing her Stetson with her gorgeous red hair flying in the breeze. Jessie scrunching her nose when she'd argued with her brother at the town meeting. Jessie shivering after she'd nearly been shot and killed.

Her rosy lips parted and inviting, plump and sensual, so ripe he'd had to have a taste. Her fingers diving into his hair as she dragged his mouth closer for a kiss. Her tongue flickering out to meet his, her body quivering beneath his touch. Her skin glistening with the moisture from his tongue. Her nipples hard and thrusting upward in need of his mouth.

But another image replaced those sensual ones—
Jessie tied and bound, Shane Tolbert's gun pressed to
her head. Shane pulling the trigger and killing her just
as he had Marcie, Daniel and Billy.

Panic threatened to immobilize him, but he inhaled
sharply and wrestled with his temper. He had to shut out
the images. Stay sharp and focused.

Save Jessie, or he wouldn't care if he lived to see
another day himself.

Shadows flickered off the giant oaks as he scanned
the riverbank in case Tolbert had decided to lay a trap.

Or in case he'd already killed Jessie and planned to
dump her body into the Colorado River.

Fear and fury raged through him at the thought. If he
had killed Jessie, he'd not only arrest the bastard, he'd
make him suffer first.

He finally spotted the cabin through the thicket of
mesquites and oaks, and saw Tolbert's car parked at an
angle in the overgrown weed-choked yard. A quick
visual of the perimeter, but he saw no one outside.

Mentally he debated his tactics. Sneak up on the
house and look inside, or call out to Tolbert and lure him
outdoors in the open away from Jessie?

He didn't have time to second-guess himself. He
inched through the woods toward the house, but the
front door opened, and Tolbert appeared in the doorway.

The deputy stood ramrod straight, his brows furrowed as he searched the yard and riverbank. Cabe
ducked behind a tree, holding his gun at the ready, then
peered around the massive tree trunk. His lungs constricted as Tolbert dragged a burlap bag from the

inside and hauled it across the yard toward the river a few feet away.

God, no… He was too late.

Tolbert had already killed Jessie.

A soul-deep ache gripped his chest in a vise. No…he couldn't be too late. Jessie had to be alive.

He needed her. Wanted her.

Loved her.

Grief clogged his throat, threatening to spill over. But Tolbert shoved the bag into the river, jerking him back to reality.

Dammit, he couldn't let Tolbert escape. Wielding his gun, he ran through the woods until he reached the clearing near the river.

"Stop!" he shouted. "Don't move, Tolbert."

Tolbert swung around and fired his weapon. Cabe felt the bullet skim his left arm, and cursed, then jumped behind an oak to dodge the next shot.

"Dammit, Tolbert, you aren't going to get away with this," he growled. "The sheriff knows you killed Marcie. Even your father knows the truth."

"You stupid Indian," Shane yelled. "I'll kill you and then I'll leave this godforsaken town, and no one will ever find me."

"The Rangers will track you down," Cabe shouted as he wove through the trees to close the distance between them.

Adrenaline pumped his blood, and he launched forward and fired at Tolbert.

Tolbert cursed and fired again, but Cabe released another round, this time hitting Tolbert in the shoulder and the knee. Tolbert went down in pain and dropped the gun as he grabbed his chest.

Cabe threw himself at Tolbert, knocking him backward. But Tolbert was strong and fought back, and managed to land a blow to Cabe's belly.

The punch only riled his anger, and his need to make Tolbert suffer, and Cabe hit Tolbert dead-on in his injured shoulder. Tolbert shouted an obscenity, and Cabe slammed his foot into the man's bleeding kneecap. Tolbert buckled with a moan, and Cabe pinned him with his body.

Out of the corner of his eye, he saw Jessie's body begin to float, then sink into the raging river, slamming against the jagged rocks with the force of the current.

Dammit, he had to hurry.

Every second that passed meant Jessie was sinking deeper into the icy water. If she was alive, she wouldn't be for long.

He grabbed his gun from the dirt, and pointed it in Tolbert's face. "Move again and I'll blow your damn head off."

Shane stilled, his eyes feral and dawning with the recognition that he had been caught.

Cabe straddled him, the gun still firmly jammed into the bastard's face as he yanked his handcuffs from his back pocket. Then he forced Tolbert to roll over facedown, and clicked the handcuffs around his wrists. Determined to make sure Tolbert didn't escape, he dragged him over to the porch edge, found some rope on the porch and tied his arms and feet to the wood posts.

"You son of a bitch," Tolbert spat. "You can't send me to jail."

"You're not just going to jail," Cabe growled. "You're going to be sitting on death row."

"It's too late to save your girlfriend," Tolbert muttered.

Hating the man with every fiber of his being, Cabe rolled his hands into a fist and punched Shane in the face again, this time so hard the sound of bones crunching rent the air.

Blood oozed from his shoulder wound and knee, and Shane's eyes turned buggy as he faded into unconsciousness. The urge to finish him off clawed at Cabe.

But fear for Jessie rattled him into action.

Sweat poured down his neck as he sprinted toward the riverbank. He scanned the surface, but he didn't see her.

Stowing his weapon beneath a jagged rock at the river's edge, he threw off his jacket and boots, then scanned the river again. He finally spotted the top of the burlap bag floating downstream, but most of her body was submerged.

Praying Shane had lied, that Jessie wasn't dead, he dove into the water. The current swept him toward some jutting rocks, but he put his head down and swam with all his might, heading downstream toward Jessie. One stroke, two, a rock jabbed his thigh, others battered his body as the current raged on.

Ignoring the pain, he increased his speed, channeling all his energy into reaching Jessie. Precious seconds passed, but he forced himself to believe that she was still alive.

Driving himself harder, he finally reached her. Diving

beneath the water, he pushed her body above the surface. Panting for air, he secured her under his arm and swam toward the riverbank.

Rocks pounded them, and the current was relentless, but a minute later he managed to reach the riverbank. He rolled her to the edge, then climbed out and hauled her body to a clearing. His chest ached for air, his body thrumming from exertion as he ripped open the top of the bag and tore it down the center.

Jessie lay inside, bound and gagged, her eyes closed.

God, no…

She wasn't breathing.

Chapter Sixteen

Cabe's life flashed before his eyes as he stared at Jessie's lifeless body.

You have your job, Cabe.

That was all that had ever mattered before. But suddenly that job meant nothing without Jessie to share his life with.

If only he hadn't left her alone. If he'd made her go with him...

No, he couldn't give up now.

He punched in Hardin's number, at the same time retrieving a knife from his pocket and slicing Jessie's bindings. Then he jerked the gag from her mouth, hoping that would allow her oxygen. "I'm almost there," Cabe said. "I've got Tolbert, but Jessie's in trouble," he shouted to Hardin. "Get an ambulance up to Tolbert's place ASAP."

He didn't wait on a response. He tilted Jessie's head back, checked her air passageway, then leaned over and began CPR. Sweat trickled down his neck as he blew air into her lungs and pumped her heart.

Agonizing seconds crawled by as he counted compressions. "Come on, Jessie, you can't die on me. I love you, dammit."

One, two, three, another breath, over and over and over. "Jessie, sweetheart, I need you. Come back to me."

The breeze picked up, rattling the trees and tossing leaves across the ground. The sound of the river slapping the embankment echoed around him, a reminder that Jessie had been lost to it moments before.

He lowered his head, blew another breath into her mouth, then stroked her cheek. But she lay limp, her body cold, stiff, unmoving, and terror clogged his throat. Had he fallen for Jessie only to lose her?

JESSIE FELT COLD. She was drowning. Her head ached, her body hurt, she couldn't move. And it was dark…so dark.

She hated the darkness.

But slowly a light invaded that darkness. The sound of a gruff voice echoed in the distance. Strong hands were beating on her chest, and a warm mouth closed over hers, blowing air into her lungs. Air she needed desperately to claw her way from the endless sea of darkness.

She had to fight her way back. Cabe was calling her. And her father needed her…

A sharp burning sensation climbed from her stomach to her throat, and her belly clenched and spasmed.

He pounded her chest again, and suddenly she felt the surge of water coming back up. Choking and coughing, she slowly opened her eyes, and Cabe angled her head sideways while she purged the water from her lungs.

She lifted her hand and clutched at him, and he

patted her back. "That's good, Jessie, that's good, baby. Let it out."

She spat out the water, dragging in a breath, trembling and shivering.

Cabe slid his arms around her, then pulled her to him, rocking her back and forth. The ambulance wailed in the distance, and he tried to warm her until the medics arrived. Then the ambulance screeched up, the medics raced toward them with a stretcher.

She hated hospitals.

She wanted Cabe to go with her. But his hand slipped away from her as the medics carried her to the ambulance.

TWO DAYS LATER, Cabe, Wyatt, Livvy and Reed met to tie up the details of the case.

Cabe requested a meeting of the townspeople, and once again, the room was packed, the room divided with the Caucasian and Native American factions.

Mayor Sadler called the meeting to order, and demanded that the two groups be quiet, then turned the meeting over to Cabe.

"Deputy Tolbert has been arrested for multiple counts of murder," Cabe said. "He confessed to killing Marcie, Daniel Taabe and Billy Whitley and will be going to prison for the rest of his life. Charla is being moved to a psychiatric unit and will spend the rest of her life locked up as well."

"What about our land?" Ellie Penateka asked.

"With Charla's testimony regarding the illegal land deal, the land will be returned to the Native American faction."

Trace Becker remained quiet, almost contrite as he sat beside Collier.

"Will charges be filed against Jonah?" Ellie pressed.

"No. Evidence suggests that Jonah did not know about the impropriety. Also, on his behalf, Jessie made arrangements to allow the Native American factions access to much-needed water on the Becker land."

Rumbles of questions began, but he quickly silenced them. "It's a win-win situation for everyone, Ellie. This town needs to work together, and the Beckers have taken the first step. Hopefully, others will follow their example, and today will mark the beginning of peace in Comanche Creek."

Clapping and shouts of agreement echoed through the room, and Cabe felt a sense of relief that he had managed to do the impossible—solve the case and bridge the gap between the two factions in his hometown.

But he couldn't have done it without Jessie. He wove through the crowd toward her, his chest swelling with love and admiration for her. But he still hadn't been able to confess his feelings. Still wasn't sure how he could handle a relationship, or if he'd be any good at it.

And Jessie deserved the best of everything.

She smiled at him, and his heart melted. "Everyone seems pleased, Cabe. And you deserve the credit here, not me."

"You played a big part by meeting with the Natives, Jessie. I meant what I said. You are an excellent role model."

A blush stained her cheeks, but an underlying

sadness still lay in her eyes. "I'm just glad they don't hate my father anymore. Now, if he'd only get better."

He wanted to promise her that Jonah would recover, but he wasn't certain about the man's condition. Still, he wanted to try something. "I'm going to visit my father, Jessie." He paused, a tightening in his belly.

"Oh, Cabe," Jessie said softly. "I'm glad you're going to reconcile with him."

He nodded. "We'll see."

Pleasure lit her eyes but a wariness remained also. He'd hurt her when she'd confessed that she loved him and he hadn't reciprocated.

He wanted to. In fact, he itched to take her back to her place and make love to her, but he had to speak with his father first.

"I'll see you again before you leave town?" Jessie asked.

He cleared his throat, then gave a clipped nod, but didn't trust his voice to speak, so simply walked outside to his car.

Memories of his family and his cultural teachings suffused him as he drove to the reservation. Pleasant memories mixed with others that troubled him, but the values and traditions he'd been taught as a child had shaped him into the man he'd become.

So had the hard lessons.

He parked the SUV, and walked across the limestone rocks, solemn and respectful as he approached his father, Quannah Navarro. His father had been named in honor of a great chief.

His hair had grayed and lay in a long braid down his

back, his sun-bronzed weathered skin looked leathery and wrinkled, but deep spiritual beliefs and strength still emanated from him.

Quannah didn't bother to look up. He had probably known Cabe was coming. He seemed to posses a sixth sense that had been almost eerie.

Except he'd believed the Big Medicine Ceremony would save Simon, and it had failed.

"Cabe, my son, I've been expecting you."

Cabe dropped to the ground, then sat cross-legged beside his father and the fire. He addressed him with the Comanche word for *father*. "Ap. You heard what happened in town?"

"Yes." Folding his gnarled hands, his father turned toward Cabe, his gaze intent as he studied Cabe. "You bridged the gap between our people and the others. Comanche Creek will change because of you, my son. For that, I am proud."

Emotions threatened to choke Cabe. His father had never praised him before.

"I knew that you would do great things, Cabe," his father said. "You are strong, brave and understand the old ways and the new."

Cabe nodded. Maybe he'd had to leave and then return to Comanche Creek to appreciate his heritage. "There is one more problem," Cabe said. "The land has been returned to the Comanche Nation, but there were angry spirits on the burial grounds."

"Yes."

"Jonah Becker has been ill lately," Cabe said. "Jessie

said he insisted that he was hearing ghosts, that the spirits were tormenting him."

"His actions disturbed the spirits, so they have been haunting him."

Cabe nodded. He'd never thought he'd ask his father for help, but Jonah's illness was tormenting Jessie. "Is there any way to put the spirits to rest and free Jonah?"

A smile curved his father's mouth, and he pushed his frail body to his feet. "Yes, my son. We will use meditation and perform the ancient ritual. Then there will be peace."

Cabe nodded. Then Jessie would be happy.

And her happiness was the most important thing in the world to Cabe.

ANXIETY NEEDLED JESSIE as she rode out to the sacred burial land.

Linda, who'd come back to work for her, had phoned to say that Cabe and an older Native American man were performing some kind of Native ceremony on the property.

Firebird cantered up to the site, and she slid from her palomino, but kept her distance and she watched from the shadows as they lit a fire and chanted to the heavens. Cabe had dressed in Native attire, the feather headdress accentuating his strong cheekbones and bronzed coloring.

She watched, mesmerized by the beauty of their movements, intrigued by the sound of their ancient language.

And Cabe... He was so damn sexy she wanted to eat him alive.

Yet she understood the spiritual significance as well as the importance of this shared moment with his father and dared not interrupt. More than anything, she wanted Cabe to make peace with his past, to reconcile with his father.

And she wanted him to know that she respected his culture and would support his choices. Even if it meant leaving her forever.

Although she'd doubted Cabe's ability to sense the spirits when she'd first met him, she believed now that he had actually heard and felt them.

Suddenly a shimmering glow radiated over the land like some kind of magic dust had been sprinkled over the terrain, and the whisper of the breeze—or ancient voices—rose in the wind.

Jessie stilled, mesmerized by the beautiful picture and the rhythm of Cabe's and his father's voices mingling with the spirits.

A heartbeat later, the earth quieted, the glow settled like a blanket over the land, and Cabe paused, opened his eyes and looked up at her.

Jessie's heart swelled with longing and with love. She'd never thought she could care so much about another person. But it wasn't the infatuation that her mother harbored over man after man. Jessie's love was unselfish and would last forever.

In fact, she loved Cabe enough to let him go if that was what he wanted. He was like a wild untamed mustang who needed to run free.

And she would not take away that freedom.

CABE SENSED THE UNCERTAINTY in Jessie's reaction as she watched him and his father. He'd known the moment she'd arrived, had intentionally not spoken to her, gauging her reaction to his customs and his father.

Now that he'd reconnected with Quannah and the Comanches, he regretted the time he'd lost. He wanted his father and the Comanche beliefs to be a part of his life, a part of his family's life.

If Jessie would have him and make that family with him.

But would her father accept him?

Quannah looked drained, and Cabe silently vowed to return to speak to Jessie, then drove his father back to the reservation, thanked him and gave him a hug.

"It will work out with your woman," his father said, as if he'd read Cabe's mind. "You have my blessings, son."

Cabe shook his hand. "Thank you for putting the souls to peace, Ap." He only hoped that doing so had healed Jessie's father.

"Before you go, I have something to give you." Cabe followed his father to his hogan, where he handed him a beaded pouch.

"This belonged to your grandmother. It is yours now."

Cabe's chest clenched as he removed the silver-and-garnet ring. It was decades old, handcrafted by his ancestors. It might be considered an artifact, was priceless, a part of his family's heritage.

"Give it to your wife-to-be," Quannah said. "Then she will be one with us."

Cabe nodded. He only hoped Jessie would accept it, and that Jonah didn't cause problems. Jessie's family was too important to her for him to come between them.

He carefully stowed it back in the pouch and headed to the Jeep.

His pulse raced as he drove to the Becker land. As he expected, he found Jessie at the main house. When he entered, sounds of joy echoed from Jonah's study.

Lolita bustled out with a smile and welcomed him. "*Sí,* Ranger Navarro. It is a blessed day. Mr. Becker has come back to us. He is his old self again." She suddenly reached up, cupped his face in her hands and kissed both his cheeks. "Miss Jessie told me what you did. You have cured him. It's a miracle! I get champagne for us to celebrate!"

Cabe grinned at her excitement, and hoped that Jessie and her father would both welcome him. Perspiration dotted his hands as he knocked on the study door and pushed the door open. "Jessie?"

Her beaming smile greeted him. "Cabe, come in. My father has had a radical recovery."

He entered, filled with trepidation over Jonah Becker's reaction to him. The man he'd met before had been ill, disoriented, but the real Jonah was an unscrupulous businessman.

"Jessie, Mr. Becker."

Jonah gave him a wary look, but waved him in. Jessie introduced him, and he extended his hand. "Mr. Becker, we met once, but it's nice to see that you're feeling better."

"My daughter tells me that I owe my recovery to you. That you solved the murders around here, saved her life, and that you and your father exorcised the spirits from my land."

He gritted his teeth. "We didn't exorcise them," Cabe

said, protective of his cultural beliefs. "We helped the spirits find peace. And you aided in doing that by returning the land to them."

Jonah shrugged. "Yes, you're right. It did belong to them." He slid a protective arm around Jessie. "I want to thank you for protecting and saving my daughter. You did a good job, Ranger Navarro."

Cabe glanced at Jessie. Love for him shone in her eyes, but there was an acceptance there as well. She would not beg him to love her or guilt him into being with her.

Her unselfishness only made his love grow stronger. And it gave him courage. She'd been right when she'd accused him of running before.

He didn't intend to run now.

"I did do my job," he admitted, then squared his shoulders. He faced hardened criminals every day. Why was it so damn difficult to confess that he loved someone, to open up his heart? "But, sir, it wasn't just my job. I care for your daughter."

It was an old-fashioned thing to do, to ask for Jonah's permission. Perhaps even lame. But tradition and family ties mattered, and he would never forget it again.

Sweat beaded on his neck, but he told himself Jessie was important enough for him to take a chance. Although if her father answered no, then he had no idea what he'd do.

"I see." Jonah pinned him with his eyes. "And your intentions, Sergeant Navarro?"

Cabe flexed his hands, trying to shake off his nerves. "I love your daughter, Mr. Becker. And I'd very much like to ask you for her hand in marriage."

Shock flashed across Jessie's face, then a brilliant smile that made his heart pound. She was just as uncertain about her father's reaction as he was, but she took a step toward him, offering hope.

Jonah gave him a long assessing look, then turned to Jessie. "I believe that decision is up to my daughter. Jessie?"

"Dad, I love Cabe," Jessie said softly. "And I would like your blessing."

Emotions glittered in Jonah's eyes. "I love you, too, Jessie. I always have." He pulled her into a hug, and tears trickled down Jessie's face.

"Thank you, Dad."

Jonah wiped at his own eyes, then cut his gaze toward Cabe. "But if you hurt her, Navarro, you'll deal with me."

"Yes, sir." Cabe finally breathed. "You have my word, sir, that I will love her with all my heart and protect her with my life."

He reached for Jessie's hand, pulled the beaded leather pouch from his pocket, then dropped to his knee. "Jessie, I love you. And if you'll do me the honor of marrying me, I will respect you, cherish you and love you for the rest of my life."

More tears filled Jessie's eyes, tears of joy. "Cabe, oh, yes. Of course, I'll marry you."

His hand shook as he slipped the ring from the pouch, then held it out to her. "It isn't a diamond, but it belonged to my grandmother and has been passed down through my family for generations." He hesitated. "My father said it will symbolize us and the joining of our families and cultures."

"It's beautiful," Jessie whispered. "Absolutely perfect."

His heart swelled as he slipped it on her finger.

An excited laugh came from her, then she launched herself into his arms. Her lips met his, and he kissed her tenderly, passionately, the pent-up need over the past two days rising to taunt him.

Lolita bobbed in with a bottle of champagne, and they pulled apart long enough to toast Jonah and their upcoming marriage. But one toast, and the secret, sultry smile Jessie graced him with indicated she was ready to be alone.

His sex hardened, the need to make love to her overpowering as they rushed back to her cabin and fell into bed.

They made love like teenagers, like lovers, like newlyweds, like a couple who had been destined to be together forever.

And he promised her that they would.

* * * * *

Harlequin offers a romance for every mood!
See below for a sneak peek
from our paranormal romance line,
Silhouette® Nocturne™.
Enjoy a preview of REUNION
by USA TODAY bestselling author
Lindsay McKenna.

Aella closed her eyes and sensed a distinct shift, like movement from the world around her to the unseen world.

She opened her eyes. And had a slight shock at the man standing ten feet away. He wasn't just any man. Her heart leaped and pounded. He reminded her of a fierce warrior from an ancient civilization. Incan? She wasn't sure but she felt his deep power and masculinity.

I'm Aella. Are you the guardian of this sacred site? she asked, hoping her telepathy was strong.

Fox's entire body soared with joy. Fox struggled to put his personal pleasure aside.

Greetings, Aella. I'm the assistant guardian to this sacred area. You may call me Fox. How can I be of service to you, Aella? he asked.

I'm searching for a green sphere. A legend says that the Emperor Pachacuti had seven emerald spheres created for the Emerald Key necklace. He had seven of his priestesses and priests travel the world to hide these spheres from evil forces. It is said that when all seven spheres are found, restrung and worn, that Light will return to the Earth. The fourth sphere is here, at your sacred site. Are you aware of it? Aella held her breath. She loved looking at him, especially his sensual mouth. The desire to kiss him came out of nowhere.

Fox was stunned by the request. *I know of the Emerald Key necklace because I served the emperor at the time it was created. However, I did not realize that one of the spheres is here.*

Aella felt sad. Why? Every time she looked at Fox, her heart felt as if it would tear out of her chest. *May I stay in touch with you as I work with this site?* she asked.

Of course. Fox wanted nothing more than to be here with her. To absorb her ephemeral beauty and hear her speak once more.

Aella's spirit lifted. What *was* this strange connection between them? Her curiosity was strong, but she had more pressing matters. In the next few days, Aella knew her life would change forever. How, she had no idea….

Look for REUNION
by USA TODAY *bestselling author*
Lindsay McKenna,
available April 2010,
only from Silhouette® Nocturne™.

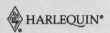

HARLEQUIN *Presents*

2 Stories in 1

HER MEDITERRANEAN PLAYBOY

Sexy and dangerous—he wants you in his bed!

The sky is blue, the azure sea is crashing
against the golden sand and the sun is hot.

The conditions are perfect for
a scorching Mediterranean seduction
from two irresistible untamed playboys!

Indulge your senses with these two delicious stories

A MISTRESS AT THE ITALIAN'S COMMAND
by Melanie Milburne

ITALIAN BOSS, HOUSEKEEPER MISTRESS
by Kate Hewitt

Available April 2010 from Harlequin Presents!

www.eHarlequin.com

HP12910

HARLEQUIN® *Romance*®

ROMANCE, RIVALRY
AND A FAMILY REUNITED

THE BRIDES *of* BELLA ROSA

William Valentine and his beloved wife, Lucia, live
a beautiful life together, but when his former love Rosa
and the secret family they had together resurface,
an instant rivalry is formed. Can these families
get through the past and come together as one?

Step into the world of Bella Rosa
beginning this April with

Beauty and the Reclusive Prince
by
RAYE MORGAN

Eight volumes to collect and treasure!

LARGER-PRINT BOOKS!

GET 2 FREE LARGER-PRINT NOVELS

PLUS 2 FREE GIFTS!

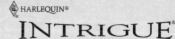

HARLEQUIN®

INTRIGUE®

Breathtaking Romantic Suspense

YES! Please send me 2 FREE LARGER-PRINT Harlequin Intrigue® novels and my 2 FREE gifts (gifts are worth about $10). After receiving them, if I don't wish to receive any more books, I can return the shipping statement marked "cancel." If I don't cancel, I will receive 6 brand-new novels every month and be billed just $4.74 per book in the U.S. or $5.74 per book in Canada. That's a saving of over 15% off the cover price! It's quite a bargain! Shipping and handling is just 50¢ per book in the U.S. and 75¢ per book in Canada.* I understand that accepting the 2 free books and gifts places me under no obligation to buy anything. I can always return a shipment and cancel at any time. Even if I never buy another book from Harlequin, the two free books and gifts are mine to keep forever.

199 HDN E4EY 399 HDN E4FC

Name _____ (PLEASE PRINT)

Address _____ Apt. #

City _____ State/Prov. _____ Zip/Postal Code

Signature (if under 18, a parent or guardian must sign)

Mail to the **Harlequin Reader Service:**
IN U.S.A.: P.O. Box 1867, Buffalo, NY 14240-1867
IN CANADA: P.O. Box 609, Fort Erie, Ontario L2A 5X3

Not valid for current subscribers to Harlequin Intrigue Larger-Print books.

Are you a subscriber to Harlequin Intrigue books and want to receive the larger-print edition? Call 1-800-873-8635 today!

* Terms and prices subject to change without notice. Prices do not include applicable taxes. N.Y. residents add applicable sales tax. Canadian residents will be charged applicable provincial taxes and GST. Offer not valid in Quebec. This offer is limited to one order per household. All orders subject to approval. Credit or debit balances in a customer's account(s) may be offset by any other outstanding balance owed by or to the customer. Please allow 4 to 6 weeks for delivery. Offer available while quantities last.

Your Privacy: Harlequin Books is committed to protecting your privacy. Our Privacy Policy is available online at www.eHarlequin.com or upon request from the Reader Service. From time to time we make our lists of customers available to reputable third parties who may have a product or service of interest to you. If you would prefer we not share your name and address, please check here. ☐

Help us get it right—We strive for accurate, respectful and relevant communications. To clarify or modify your communication preferences, visit us at www.ReaderService.com/consumerchoice.

HILP10

SPECIAL EDITION

INTRODUCING A BRAND-NEW MINISERIES FROM *USA TODAY* BESTSELLING AUTHOR

KASEY MICHAELS

SECOND-CHANCE BRIDAL

At twenty-eight, widowed single mother Elizabeth Carstairs thinks she's left love behind forever....until she meets Will Hollingsbrook. Her sons' new baseball coach is the handsomest man she's ever seen—and the more time they spend together, the more undeniable the connection between them. But can Elizabeth leave the past behind and open her heart to a second chance at love?

FIND OUT IN

SUDDENLY A BRIDE

Available in April
wherever books are sold.

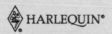

INTRIGUE®

COMING NEXT MONTH

Available April 13, 2010